"STARSHIP CAPTAINS ARE LIKE CHILDREN," SCOTTY SAID IN AN AVUNCULAR TONE.

"They want everything right now and they want it their way. The secret is to give them what **they** need, not what they want."

Scott's advice went completely against the grain of Geordi's personality. "I told Captain Picard I'd have that analysis done in an hour," he said firmly.

Scott grinned conspiratorially. "An' how long will it *really* take you?"

Geordi was puzzled now—genuinely puzzled. "An hour," he replied.

The other man seemed shocked. "Ye didnae tell him how long it was *really* going to take."

Geordi was irritated—and getting more so by the second. "Of course I did."

Scott rolled his eyes in mock disappointment. "Laddie, laddie, laddie. Ye've got a lot to learn if ye want them to think of ye as a miracle worker."

Look for STAR TREK Fiction from Pocket Books

Star Trek: The Original Series

Star Trek: The Next Generation

Most Pocket Books are available at special quantity discounts for bulk purchases for sales promotions, premiums or fund raising. Special books or book excerpts can also be created to fit specific needs.

For details write the office of the Vice President of Special Markets, Pocket Books, 1230 Avenue of the Americas, New York, New York 10020.

STAR TREK®
THE NEXT GENERATION™

RELICS

**A Novel by MICHAEL JAN FRIEDMAN
Based on the Television Episode
Story and Teleplay by RON MOORE**

POCKET BOOKS
New York   London   Toronto   Sydney   Tokyo   Singapore

An *Original* Publication of POCKET BOOKS

POCKET BOOKS, a division of Simon & Schuster Inc.
1230 Avenue of the Americas, New York, NY 10020

STAR TREK is a Registered Trademark of
Paramount Pictures.

This book is published by Pocket Books, a division of
Simon & Schuster Inc., under exclusive license from
Paramount Pictures.

ISBN: 0-671-86476-9

First Pocket Books printing November 1992

10 9 8 7 6 5 4 3 2 1

POCKET and colophon are registered trademarks of
Simon & Schuster Inc.

Printed in the U.S.A.

For little Jared,
the newest addition to the crew

Acknowledgments

It's funny how these things work out.

It's only recently that I've begun attending Star Trek conventions. So while some of my fellow writers are like *that* with some of the stars we've come to know and love, I've only had occasion to speak with one or two of them.

At Toronto Trek VI, however, I had the pleasure of meeting Jimmy Doohan. (I'd normally be inclined toward the more respectful "James," but "Jimmy" seems to fit him a whole lot better.)

The con chairpersons had thrown a little party to kick off the weekend-long event. When I arrived, I scanned the crowd, hoping to catch a glimpse of Mr. Doohan. No sign as yet, though.

Then there was a commotion at the door, and in bustles Jimmy with a pouchful of flexible refrigerator magnets—looking for all the world like Santa Claus in the off season. The magnets had a cartoon image of our beloved Montgomery Scott—laying back in an easy chair, feet up, a big smile on his face—while the intercom system blasts: "Beam me up, Scotty! There's no intelligent life down here!"

In my experience, few media personalities live up to their billing. Jimmy Doohan, on the other hand, was everything I'd heard he was—a man of inexhaustible charm and wit, an actor's actor and one hell of a nice guy. And in an age when performers like to distance themselves from their roles, Jimmy embraced his Scotty persona like an old friend.

Shortly after I got home, I got a call from another man who lives up to his billing: Dave Stern, Pocket Books' Star Trek editor. "How'd you like to do a novelization?" he asked. And since I'd been lobbying to do one for some time, I said, "Sure. What's it about and when's it due?"

What it was about was Scotty's appearance in a Next Generation episode . . . as you know by now, having seen the cover of this book. Great, I thought. It's kismet. I meet Jimmy Doohan and then I write a book about his best-known role. I'd been doing research that whole weekend in Toronto without knowing it.

As for when it was due . . . I had a whole *month*. Four and a half weeks. Thirty-one long, leisurely days. Seven hundred and forty-four hours, only some of which I would have to devote to sleep. To write a *book*. Gee, I wondered, what was I going to do with all that time on my hands?

My first impulse was to say it's impossible. Absolutely impossible. I mean, I can only write so fast.

There wasn't enough time, plain and simple—and I couldn't change the laws of physics, now could I?

Then I realized: this book was about Scotty. Of *course* it was going to have an impossible deadline. And somehow, some way, it was going to get published on time—even if I had to work my poor wee fingers down to the first knuckle.

Along the way, I found myself grateful to a few people. First and foremost to Ron Moore, for his thoughtful and moving script. Next to Mike Okuda, for advice and generosity past, present and future. And finally to Carla Mason, without whose insight and cooperation this project could never have materialized from the ether.

I hope you have half as much fun with this story as I did.

RELICS

Prologue

MONTIE SCOTT was flying free. The wind, cold and bracing, stretched the skin of his face over his young cheekbones, making him grin like a hyena. His hang glider bucked once and then again under the influence of an especially strong gust, reminding him of how weary his arms were.

But he was far from even thinking about a landing. Tired as they were, Scott's arms had plenty of life left in them. And he wasn't about to give up a single, blessed second of the breathtaking view hundreds of meters beneath him.

Great buttresses of gray rock. Long, green sweeps of hillside. Deep, dark cuts in the earth, breathing a scent of mystery that he could fairly smell all the way up here in the clouds.

Away off in the north, there was a steel-gray line of storm clouds bearing down on him. But they wouldn't force him out of the sky either. Experience had taught him that weather from that quarter took a while to arrive.

Freedom. It was better than anything, better than a hundred-year-old scotch, better even than the mournful song of the pipes in the dusky highlands. When one came right down to it, it was freedom that made a man feel alive . . .

"Captain Scott?"

Suddenly, the craggy, green vistas below him seemed to melt away. Scott blinked once, twice, and saw the long, narrow face of Matt Franklin looming in front of him, his straw-yellow hair plastered tight to his skull in the fashion of the day.

"Huh?" said Scott. It took him a moment more to get his bearings—to realize that he was in a ship's library, and that there was an active monitor in front of him. And that he'd dozed off.

Unfortunately, he was doing more and more of that these days. And it annoyed the hell out of him.

Ensign Franklin smiled. "Sorry, sir. I didn't mean to disturb your nap."

"I was *nae* takin' a nap," Scott protested. And then: "What brings ye down here, anyway? Is somethin' wrong?"

Franklin shook his head reassuringly. "Nothing serious, sir. It's just that there's a little problem with the warp drive, and we're going to have to drop down to impulse in a few minutes. The captain thought all the passengers should know—so you won't be alarmed when you feel the deceleration."

Scott looked at Franklin askance. "A *little* problem? Are ye certain o' that?"

The ensign nodded, his smile broadening. "Nothing to worry about, sir. Just a slight overload in one of the plasma transfer conduits."

The older man started to get up. "Well, I suppose I could take a look at it . . ."

Franklin laid a gentle hand on Scott's shoulder. "No need, sir. Really. I know you used to be an engineer yourself, but Lieutenant Sachs has it under control."

Scott's enthusiasm subsided as he noted the firmness in the ensign's eyes. "All right, then," he sighed. "As long as he feels he can handle it."

In an obvious attempt to change the subject, Franklin pointed to the monitor. "Anything interesting, sir?"

Scott shrugged. "Just an' old text—very old, in fact. I came across it when I was at the Academy."

The ensign bent closer to the screen to read the title of the thing. *"The Laws of Physics,"* he said out loud.

The older man nodded. "Aye. *The Laws o' Physics.* Came out shortly after Einstein published his *Theory of Relativity.* A remarkable book—if only as a historical artifact. No mention of gravitons, subspace or antimatter." He shook his head. "We've come a long way since the twentieth century, laddie."

Franklin chuckled. "No question about *that.* Anyway, I'll let you get back to it, sir."

Scott grunted. Truth to tell, he wasn't all that eager to return to the screen. Hell, he'd read the bloody thing about a dozen times already. He practically knew it by heart.

His daydream, on the other hand, had been exciting as all get-out. He'd forgotten how exhilarating it could be to soar over the shaggy hills of his homeland.

"Ensign," he said abruptly, freezing Franklin just shy of the door. The younger man turned around.

"Aye, sir?"

"Have ye ever been hang glidin', Mister Franklin?"

The younger man shook his head—a little sadly, Scott thought. "No, sir, I haven't." And then: "Have you?"

Scott sat back in his chair. "Since ye ask, yes. Not lately, mind ye. I'm talking forty years ago or more, before I even got accepted at the Academy."

He gestured at a chair not more than a meter away. For a moment, Franklin hesitated, and Scott scowled inwardly.

Ye're a crazy coot, Montgomery Scott. This lad's got things to do on this ship—important things. An' no time to listen to an old man spin his yarns.

But the ensign surprised him. Crossing the room, he grabbed the proffered chair, turned it around and straddled it.

If the lad wasn't genuinely interested, Scott mused, he sure didn't let on to it. Either way, Scott was grateful.

"Ye see," he began, "I was born and reared in Scotland—as if ye couldnae tell. And my uncle—on my mother's side, that is—was a hang glider from way back . . ."

Twenty minutes later, Scott was still regaling the younger man with tales of his airborne exploits. But he didn't realize it until he happened to glance at the digital timekeeper at the bottom left of his monitor.

"Damn," he breathed. "I've kept ye a mite longer than I meant to."

Franklin grinned. "That's all right. I'm off-duty."

Ah. Well, that explained why he hadn't made tracks yet.

"And besides," said the ensign, "I'm really enjoying myself." He leaned forward over the backrest of his chair. "But what I'd really like to hear about is the *Enterprise*. You know—what it was like to be on the most famous vessel in the fleet."

Scott grinned back. "What it was like?" He shook his head. "It's hard to describe, actually. I mean, what we *did* is in the computer records—the missions we carried out, the civilizations we visited. But what it was *like* . . . that had more to do with the men and women who served alongside me. And o' course, the ship *herself*."

"Captain Kirk?" Franklin prodded.

"Finest man I ever met, bar none. The finest commanding officer, the finest friend. And a fair hand with the ladies, to boot."

"Commander Spock?"

Scott chuckled. "Like any other Vulcan—but more so. If ye're in the jaws o' hell, and ye can only choose one man to pull ye out . . . Spock's that man."

"Dr. McCoy?"

"A real crabapple . . . until ye get to know him, and then ye'd walk through fire for him. Saved my life more times than I've got fingers and toes."

Scott took a breath of memory, savored it and let it out. Those were the days, all right. There were adventures before and since that time and some fond remembrances from those times as well. But the *Enterprise* . . .

"Captain Scott?"

He'd almost forgotten that Franklin was sitting in front of him. "Aye, lad?"

"This is going to sound funny, but . . ."

"Spit it out, Ensign. No need to mince words with me."

Franklin straightened, a little surprised by the sudden authority in Scott's voice. "Well, sir, pardon me for saying so, but—"

"Ye're mincin' words again, laddie."

Finally, it came out: "You don't seem like the type to be headed for the Norpin Five colony, sir. I mean, I've served on this transport for more than a year now, and I've seen my share of retirees. And somehow, you just don't fit the bill."

"Ahh." Scott dismissed the idea with a wave of his hand. "It's nice o' ye to say so, Mr. Franklin. But ye're wrong—dead wrong. I've worked my fingers to the bone on Starfleet's behalf for four decades and more. No one's earned a peaceful retirement more than Montgomery Scott has. And no one's looking forward to it more, either. In fact—"

Suddenly, he felt a shudder in the deck plates below his feet. "We're droppin' out o' warp," he judged.

The ensign nodded. "Probably not for long, though."

Scott looked at him. "Because Lieutenant Sachs has everything under control."

Franklin nodded again. "That's what he said, sir."

The older man tapped his fingers on his armrest. And then, unable to contain himself any longer, he got to his feet.

"I dinnae care what Lieutenant Sachs said. I was

6

tinkerin' with warp engines before he was old enough to walk. An' I'll be damned if I dinnae at least take a *look* at what's goin' on down there."

The ensign shrugged as he got to his feet as well. He had a look of mock resignation about him. "I tried to stop you, sir. But you were just too insistent."

"Ye're bloody right I was," said Scott, heading for the exit and the corridor outside.

Captain James Armstrong sat in his command chair, scanning the starfields ahead of the *Jenolen* courtesy of his forward viewscreen, but he wasn't exactly thrilled to be there. He'd envisioned better things when he applied for admission to Starfleet Academy some twenty years ago.

It wasn't fair, he mused. He'd studied as diligently as anyone else. He'd worked hard, scoring high in every phase of cadet training. He'd held up his end of the bargain.

Sure, he'd flubbed the Kobayashi Maru test—but so had everyone else. Only one man in the annals of the Academy had beaten the no-win scenario, and that had been decades earlier.

Like the other cadets, Armstrong had hoped for adventure, for the excitement of discovery. He'd looked forward to plumbing the depths of the unknown. What he'd gotten was a transport vessel, whose only mission was to ferry Federation citizens from one world to another.

Where was the justice in that?

Here he was pushing forty, his wavy, light-brown hair graying at the temples, and all his old classmates had passed him by. Lustig was in the command chair on the *Hood,* Barrymore on the *Lexington,* DeCampo on the newly commissioned *Excalibur*—every last one of them a success.

Except for him.

And why? He couldn't say. Bad luck, maybe. A failure to be in the right place at the right time.

Sighing, he looked about his operations center—a cramped complex, which on a larger ship would have been at least three and possibly four separate facilities. This wasn't just his command center, where he sat daily, bemoaning his fate as he stared unimpressed at the viewscreen. It was also the place that housed the *Jenolen*'s warp-drive access—a crowded array of engineering consoles manned by a crowded array of engineers—and a modest, two-man transporter platform.

On the *Potemkin,* where he'd served as ensign, the transporter room alone was bigger than this. Hell, the *closets* were bigger than this.

"Ready to drop out of warp," announced tall, dark-haired Ben Sachs from his position behind the main engineering console. There were two other engineers working alongside him—the full complement of Ops center personnel.

Again, Armstrong had occasion to reflect on the inequities of his situation. On the *Potemkin,* there'd been a crew of more than four hundred. On the *Jenolen,* all he had were thirty-six—and he could probably have made due with even fewer in a pinch.

"Go ahead, Lieutenant," he told Sachs. "As we discussed, we'll proceed at full impulse while we effect repairs."

"Aye, sir," said his chief engineer—in a vaguely annoyed tone, Armstrong thought. There'd been no need to remind Sachs about maintaining impulse power; they'd only talked about it a few minutes ago.

Unfortunately, the captain wasn't required to give a whole lot of orders on the transport ship *Jenolen*— and sometimes he felt that he had to say *something*.

The vessel vibrated slightly as its warp bubble dissipated and it re-entered relativistic space. Armstrong grunted. He could almost have wished that something had gone wrong—that alarms were going off all over the place, and that it was up to his quick, resourceful mind to get them out of a situation no starship captain had ever faced before.

Not that he wished to endanger anyone— particularly the bunch of older folks headed for Norpin Five. But just once, he wanted to feel like a *real* commanding officer.

"Sir?" said Sachs, interrupting Armstrong's reverie.

"Yes, Lieutenant?" He turned to his chief engineer.

The man looked perplexed. "We're picking up a considerable amount of gravimetric interference," he noted.

His curiosity aroused, the captain got up and crossed the Ops center to stand at Sachs's side. "Gravimetric interference?" he echoed.

The engineer nodded. "And I think I've pinpointed the source of it."

"Can you give me a visual?" asked the captain.

Sachs consulted his monitors. "Yes," he said. "I believe I can."

A moment later, the image on the viewscreen

changed from that of a gently flowing river of stars to something a good deal more ominous. What Armstrong and his engineers saw was a dark, featureless ball, one that would have been difficult indeed to discern with the naked eye if not for the stars it displaced. It almost completely filled the dimensions of the screen.

Now it was the captain's turn to be annoyed. "I didn't ask for maximum magnification, Ben. Don't anticipate."

Sachs turned to him, his heavy brows raised in indignant response. "I didn't, sir. This is the lowest magnification setting we've got."

The lowest . . . ? But for the sphere to fill the viewscreen at that kind of distance . . . !

"My god," said Armstrong. "Is that thing as big as I think it is?"

The engineering chief nodded soberly. "Nearly the size of Earth's orbit around Sol."

The captain was in awe as he took a couple of steps toward the screen. It wasn't listed on any of his navigational charts.

Suddenly, a grin crossed his face. It had been a long time since he'd grinned this way; it felt strange and wonderful.

"Any idea what it is, Captain?" asked Sachs.

"None," said Armstrong. But inwardly, he knew exactly what it was . . .

His ticket to a *real* command.

As the turbolift doors opened, Scott got a view of the *Jenolen*'s operations center. Strangely, everyone seemed to be standing around, staring open-mouthed at the viewscreen.

"Remember," Ensign Franklin whispered. "I tried to talk you out of it."

"That you did," agreed the older man. But he was already craning his neck to see what everyone was so fascinated by.

It was a perfect ball hanging in space. Not a planet, but something artificial. Walking over to the nearest unoccupied engineering console, he activated it.

And saw what had the crew so intrigued. According to the numbers displayed alongside the sphere's digitized image in the console, the bloody thing was twice the size of the Sol system—and then some.

"Composition?" asked Captain Armstrong, a stocky fellow who had greeted Scott personally when the older man boarded the ship. Armstrong hadn't seemed to like his job very much—until now.

"Carbon-neutronium," responded Sachs, the engineer. "That means our sensors can't penetrate the surface. Too bad." He straightened to his full height, which made him nearly a head taller than the captain. "It would have been nice to know what's going on in there."

Armstrong frowned thoughtfully. "Then let's survey what's on the outside as closely as possible. And before we're done, if we're lucky, we'll at least be able to venture a guess as to what's *inside*."

"Aye," said Scott. "Though ye'll want to approach 'er with caution, lad. Ye never know what her makers might've had up their sleeves."

The captain must not have known Scott was there

until he spoke—because when he turned to face the older man, he seemed surprised by his presence. Immediately, his eyes sought Franklin, who just shrugged helplessly.

Finding Scott again, he said: "To what do I owe the pleasure, Captain?"

In other words, thought Scott, what the devil are *you* doing here? He put on his most casual air.

"I thought ye might need my help," he replied plainly. And then, with a gesture to the viewscreen: "And now I'm sure of it."

Armstrong's gaze locked onto Scott's. "We can handle ourselves just fine," said the captain. "As Mr. Franklin no doubt informed you."

"Aye," said the older man. "He informed me, all right. But that was before ye ran into a Dyson Sphere."

That got Armstrong's attention. "A Dy . . . I beg your pardon?"

"A Dyson Sphere," Scott repeated. And in fifty words or less, he described the theory behind such a construct. "O' course," he finished, "I cannae guarantee it's what I think it is. But it's certainly got all the earmarks of it."

"I see," said the captain. He glanced at Lieutenant Sachs. "You're familiar with such a thing?"

The engineer smiled ruefully. "Frankly, sir, I'm not. Under the circumstances . . . it might not be a bad idea for Captain Scott to remain in the Ops center. As a sort of, er . . . consultant."

Armstrong's facial muscles went taut. It was plain he didn't like the idea of needing help from a civilian —even one with a half-century's experience in

Starfleet. But if his chief engineer wasn't objecting, how could *he?*

"All right," he acquiesced. "Make yourself at home, Captain Scott."

"Scotty," the older man amended. "That's the name I answer to in an engineering room—and this is pretty near that."

Armstrong looked at him appraisingly. "Scotty it is, then."

Scott grinned. "Good. Now that we understand each other, let's get to work."

Matt Franklin felt a hand on his shoulder. Looking up from his engineering console, he saw Captain Scott peering affably at him from beneath his bushy, gray brows.

"How's our orbit, lad?"

The ensign nodded, feeling a twinge in his neck—but resolving not to complain about it. Thanks to Scott, who'd dubbed the younger man his personal assistant in their scan of the Dyson Sphere, Franklin was the envy of every nonofficer in the crew. Sure, five straight hours of close analysis had taken their toll on him. But a couple of aches and pains were a small price to pay for an opportunity that might never materialize a second time.

"Fine, sir," he replied, pointing to the relevant figures in the upper right-hand corner of his screen. "I haven't had to make a course correction in hours."

"Good," said Scott. "Nae that I would've expected otherwise; being a perfect sphere, that thing shouldn't present any magnetic aberrations. But no news is good news, I always say."

Squeezing the ensign's shoulder paternally, the older man stalked off to see how the rest of the engineering cadre was doing. Slowly but surely, he seemed to have supplanted Sachs as the individual in charge of the operation—though to Sachs's credit, he was being a good sport about it.

Just a few days ago, Matt Franklin hadn't known very much about the man called Montgomery Scott—other than what he had read. The passenger manifest had showed that Scott was a lifetime officer in Starfleet, who had served nearly all fifty-two years of his career on the fabled *Enterprise*.

He'd boarded the ship as a young engineer under Captain Pike, reached the rank of lieutenant commander under James T. Kirk and remained to train others after his captain was given an admiral's braid. In the intervening time, he'd been reunited with Kirk and his former *Enterprise* colleagues on and off, sometimes for years at a time.

All that was in the computer records. All public knowledge.

But now Franklin had had a chance to meet the man behind the career. And he was glad of it. Very glad of it.

Montgomery Scott was the kind of man you met only once in a lifetime. Someone whose capacity for invention seemed almost limitless . . . whose love for knowledge was so strong, so fierce, it sometimes seemed to be a force of nature.

Didn't Scott fix those overloaded plasma transfer circuits faster than anyone in the Ops center had believed possible—Lieutenant Sachs included? Without him, they'd still be *thinking* about approaching the sphere, not hours into the analysis already.

In a way, the man was like the Dyson Sphere itself—an anomaly, an oddity. A gem of rare quality, not to be missed on pain of great regret.

Abruptly, even as Franklin was finishing his thought, the lift doors opened and the captain stormed in. Nor did he look any happier than when he departed.

"Civilians," Armstrong muttered. "Why did I think they might actually understand? Why did I think they might be willing to tolerate a small delay for the sake of science?" He shook his head as he sat down wearily in his command chair, his voice drifting off into muttered invective.

Suppressing a smile, Franklin turned back to his monitor and scanned yet another portion of the artificial globe. Not that he expected to see much of anything, but—

Wait. His mouth went dry. What was *that*?

"You'd think we were fooling around out here," said Armstrong, his voice rising to an audible level again. "You'd think we were wasting time, not making one of the great scientific discoveries of our—"

"Captain?"

It took Franklin a moment to realize that it was *he* who had spoken up, interrupting the captain's soliloquy and drawing everyone's attention. He swallowed uncomfortably, his mouth drier than ever.

"Yes, Ensign?" asked Armstrong.

"Sir," Franklin went on, "I've found something that looks like a communications antenna."

Scott was by his side in an instant. "Aye," he confirmed. "So it does, lad." He made some adjustments in the scope of the scan. "And look—here's another. And a third. No—four. Four o' them." Turning to the captain, he said: "They look intact, too. I wouldn't be surprised if they were in working order."

A smile spread over Armstrong's face, making him look like a man who'd just gotten his heart's desire. He nodded.

"Then by all means," he said, "let's open hailing frequencies."

At one of the other engineering consoles, Communications Officer Kinski followed the captain's orders. "Hailing frequencies opened," he confirmed.

They waited. No response.

Looks were exchanged between crew members . . . between Captain Armstrong and Mr. Sachs . . . between Franklin himself and Captain Scott. The sense of expectation was almost suffocating.

And still no reply from the Dyson Sphere.

"Try again," said Armstrong, his voice a little more subdued.

"Trying," reported Kinksi.

Again, there was that expectant silence. It stretched on for too long. Franklin shook his head, disappointed.

"Damn," said the captain.

"Ye can say that again," Scott sympathized. "Fer a moment there, I really thought we might be able to raise them."

"Maybe we're giving up too soon," Sachs offered.

"The fact that they're not answering doesn't mean that they can't—or that they won't. Maybe they're just being cautious."

Scott sighed. "I dinnae think so, Lieutenant. Call it a sixth sense if ye will, but I'll bet ye a bottle o' scotch that if ye hailed from now till doomsday, ye'd have no more luck than ye're havin' now. Plain and simple, there's nobody in there."

"He's right," Armstrong joined in. "Anybody who's got the technology to build a Dyson Sphere has nothing to fear from us. If there were sentient beings inside that sphere, we'd have heard from them by now."

How could they be so sure? Franklin looked from Scott to Armstrong and back to Scott. How could they *know* beyond a doubt?

The ensign had barely finished the thought when the deck lurched beneath him and he went sprawling across it. He felt someone lifting him up as someone else spat out a question.

A second later, still a third person cried out the answer: "The power coils, sir! They've blown!"

Fortunately, Scott had been in a position to get a good grip on the engineering console when the explosion rocked them, or he'd have gone tumbling across the Ops center like Sachs and Franklin. Hanging on tight against the prospect of a second blast, he worked at his keyboard until he'd confirmed Sachs's conclusion.

The aft coils had blown all right. But how? There were half a dozen fail-safe systems to prevent something like that. And even if none of them had been working, they should have had plenty of warning from the diagnostics.

"Damage report," Armstrong called out, hanging on grimly to his command chair. And then, almost as an afterthought: "Any casualties?"

"No deaths, sir," returned Kinski, consulting his monitors. "But widespread injuries, especially in the passenger quarters."

"Extensive damage to the power conduits," announced Sachs. The man looked shaken, white as a ghost. But then, things like this didn't usually happen to transport ships. "Attempting to compensate by diverting power to the ventral relays. Give me a hand, Mr. Franklin."

That was just what Scott would have done. As young Franklin took up a position at the next console, he followed their efforts on the computer screen.

Come on, he cheered inwardly. Carry the load, ye bloody beasties.

But it only took a minute or two for Scott to see that it wasn't working—and another few seconds to see why. The damage had been more extensive than Sachs had guessed. The explosion had backed up into the warp drive—though the magnetic bottle showed no signs of giving way.

"Well?" asked the captain.

Sachs shook his head. "No response, sir. The warp engines are down." He called up another screen and cursed beneath his breath.

"What now?" prompted Armstrong. "Don't tell me the impulse engines are dead too."

"Not quite," said Scott, who'd been tracking the

status of the propulsion systems along with the chief engineer. "But they've suffered collateral damage from the coil explosion. There's nae enough power there to keep us in orbit."

The captain glared at him. "What are you saying?"

"The *Jenolen* is losing altitude," Scott explained as calmly as he could. "We're caught in th' bloody sphere's gravity well and we cannae get out."

"That can't be," insisted Armstrong. "Surely the engines can be fixed."

Sachs shook his head. "I'm afraid not. There's too much damage—and not enough time." He looked to Scott for confirmation—and got it in the form of bleak silence.

Montgomery Scott had pulled his share of rabbits out of his hat. But for once, even he was at a loss. There were lots of ways he could think of to pull the *Jenolen*'s engines together. But any of them would have taken many more hours than they had left.

The captain licked his lips. "You mean there's nothing we can do? We're just going to crash?"

It went against the older man's grain to admit it, but as he'd told Jim Kirk time and again, there was no changing the laws of physics. "Aye," he conceded. "That's about the size of it."

Armstrong's brow creased as he wrestled with the enormity of Scott's statement. "How long before impact?"

His chief engineer supplied the answer: "Seventeen minutes, thirty-five seconds, sir."

Ben Sachs was a man with modest ambitions, the product of a long line of men with modest ambitions.

Sure, he'd wanted to get into space, to tinker with a warp drive and feel the joy of having it respond to his tinkerings. But unlike his peers, he'd never aspired to serving on a Constitution-class vessel.

So when the assignment came down to replace the chief engineer of the transport ship *Jenolen,* Sachs had been happy to accept it. More than happy, in fact.

Let the other fellows work under unrelenting pressure, he'd told himself at the time. Let them walk their daily treadmills, eat their meals in a blinding hurry, lie awake at night wondering if there was some gauge they might have misread. Let them strain their brains trying to remember what attracted them to this life in the first place.

I'll be content swimming in a smaller pond, where I can take time to enjoy the view without feeling guilty about it. I'll be just fine on the good ship *Jenolen.*

Up until now, Sachs's prediction had been right on the money. He *had* been fine. He'd found the perfect, uneventful niche for himself.

And more than that, he'd found love—the perfect love only an engineer can feel for his ship. Ben Sachs had fallen head over heels for a transport vessel that no one else would have given a second look.

But in a flash, that had all changed. Now he was riding the *Jenolen* down to the dark and featureless Dyson Sphere below. And the odds of his idyllic life going on in its idyllic way—hell, going on at *all*—seemed more and more remote with each passing second.

Strangely, that didn't inspire fear in him—not really. It didn't even inspire regret. Sachs had never married, had never had children, and his parents were long gone. He wasn't leaving anyone behind.

He was going to die alongside his one true love. The romance of it appealed to him, so much so that it overshadowed the grisly fate awaiting him at the bottom of the gravity well.

"Mr. *Sachs!*"

The chief engineer shook his head and sought out the source of the shout. He found himself gaping at a narrow-eyed Montgomery Scott.

"Are ye with me or nae, lad?" asked Scott.

Sachs swallowed. "With you on what?"

The older man cursed beneath his breath. "Have ye nae been listening to a word I've said? We cannae prevent ourselves from crashing into the Dyson Sphere, but we *can* keep casualties to a minimum. That is, if we can find a half-dozen crewmen willing to stick it out here in the Ops center."

Sachs's mind raced, making up for the time during which he was distracted. After a second or two, he saw what Scott was getting at.

There were turbulence-berths in the passenger section. Strapped into them, a body would have at least a shot at survival. But here in the Ops center, where there was nothing to cushion them against the impact . . . the odds of living through the crash were a lot longer.

And yet, someone had to remain here. To use what impulse thrust was left in an attempt to slow them down. To boost the shields at just the right moment. And to maintain the ship's attitude lest it fall on its side, where structural support was the weakest.

Sachs nodded. "I get it," he said.

"Now ye're payin' attention, lad." The older man's shaggy brows knit. "The only question is who's goin' to stay and who's goin' to go."

Glances were exchanged. Feet were shuffled. Breaths were expelled.

"Well," Scott announced, "I guess I'm the most expendable one here. It makes sense for me to stick around." He looked to Sachs.

"Me too," said the engineer, drawing stares of admiration from the others. No doubt, they thought he was being brave.

They were wrong, of course. He was just caught up in his romantic madness. But he wasn't going to tell them that. If they wanted to remember him as a hero . . . what the hell, why not let them?

Captain Armstrong cleared his throat. "I'm staying as well. I'm no engineer, but I've worked closely enough with them over the years. And I can follow orders as well as anyone."

Scott smiled. "Glad to have ye aboard," he told Armstrong.

The captain smiled back, though without quite so much gusto. "Thank you, Captain Scott."

They looked around. "Any other takers?" called Sachs.

No one answered. He didn't blame them. And then, after what seemed like a long time, one hand went up.

It was Franklin's.

"I'd like to remain also," he told the chief engineer. He looked to Armstrong. "If it's all right with you, sir."

The captain regarded him for a moment, no doubt

thinking of the ensign's youth. But then, most every crewman on the *Jenolen* was young. And they needed every hand they could get.

"It's all right with me," agreed Armstrong. "And thank you, Mr. Franklin."

Turning to the others, the captain looked benevolent—understanding. When he spoke, there wasn't even a hint of recrimination in his voice.

"The rest of you should make your way to the passenger deck as quickly as possible. You don't have much time to secure yourselves."

Looking grateful, they departed into the turbolift. Sachs watched them go, envying them just a little. But there was no turning back now. He'd thrown his lot in with Captain Scott; he'd see this through to its conclusion.

"Time to impact?" asked Armstrong.

Sachs consulted his monitor again. "Twelve minutes and fifty-two seconds," he replied. "We'd better get started."

"Aye," said Scott. He addressed the chief engineer. "I hope ye dinnae mind if I direct things from here on in. After all, I've had a wee bit more experience at crash landings."

"Not at all," Sachs told him honestly. "She's all yours, sir."

Scott looked a couple of inches taller as he took charge. "Very well then. Mr. Franklin, ye've got the helm. Bring us down straight and true."

"You can count on me, sir" said the ensign.

"I'm glad to hear that," Scott remarked. He turned to Sachs. "Plot a curve with exponentially increasing thrust. But dinnae use everything we've got; we'll need some power for life support if . . . I mean *when* we make it."

"Aye," answered Sachs, never one to mince words.

Finally, Scott regarded the captain, who had come down from his command chair to stand behind one of the engineering consoles. "There will nae be a whole lot for ye to do right now," said the older man. "But when I give ye the signal, ye're to reconfigure the deflector shields—to give us maximum protection at the point of impact."

Armstrong nodded. "Standing by," he replied.

Scott took a deep breath and let it out. "No doubt," he went on, "ye're all curious as to what *I'll* be doing."

"Building up our power reserves?" ventured Franklin.

"Begging, borrowing and stealing from peripheral systems," Sachs expanded. "Cleaning out every last nook and cranny."

The older man glanced at them, deadpan. "It was sort of a rhetorical question, gentlemen. But thank ye for your help nonetheless."

Over the next few minutes, they all applied themselves to their respective tasks. Sachs found his mind remarkably clear, remarkably facile, as he first plotted and then began to execute the impulse thrust curve Scott had asked for.

When he had occasion to look up, he saw that the others were similarly absorbed in what they were doing. There were no signs of panic. The engineer smiled, glad that what were probably his last moments would be in the company of professionals.

Abruptly, the ship began to slip its axis. Franklin muttered a curse.

"Ease her back, Ensign," said Scott, his voice calm as a tree-shrouded pond. "We're in no hurry."

Responding to the older man's demeanor as much as his advice, Franklin made the necessary corrections. On Sachs's screen, the *Jenolen* righted herself.

"Well done," Scott observed. "Now steady as she goes."

Two and a half minutes. Two. One and a half.

Sixty seconds.

As Franklin held the ship upright, Sachs applied thrust in ever-increasing amounts. Nonetheless, they were accelerating, drawn to the sphere by its uncommonly strong gravitational field.

"All right," said Scott. They were approaching the thirty-second mark. "Bring those shields around, Captain."

Armstrong did as he was told. "Shields in place," he confirmed. "We're as protected as we'll ever be."

They'd done all they could, Sachs mused. The rest was in the lap of the gods. He held onto his console.

Twenty seconds. Fifteen. Ten.

Sachs found it hard to swallow. Good-bye, *Jenolen*.

Five. Four. Three. Two . . .

One.

For a second or two, Scott didn't know what had hit him, or even where he was. Then consciousness came swarming back like a thundering river in flood.

The Ops center was a flaming, sparking inferno. Smoke was everywhere, making it almost impossible to see. He coughed painfully.

But he was *alive*. He was bruised and battered and there was an aching tenderness in his left arm, but despite the odds he'd come through. And if a man his age could survive, there were probably others who'd survived as well.

Scott winced. There was something in his eye. Dabbing at it gingerly, his fingers came away with a sticky film of blood on them.

Bloody, he remarked inwardly, but unbowed—just like the poem. His mind started to drift back to the highlands, and a lass who liked nothing better than poetry . . . except *him* . . .

No, he told himself firmly, shaking himself out of his reverie. None o' that. I may have suffered a concussion, but I cannae let that stop me. I've got to focus on the task ahead—that being to see who else might be alive and then assess the damage to the ship.

Out of the corner of his eye, he noticed something. A man's hand, not more than a meter away . . . moving ever so slightly? Or was it just his imagination? He pulled himself over to it as best he could.

"Laddie?" he said tentatively. He could barely hear himself over the popping sound coming from a ruined console.

No answer. He crept a little closer—past the hand to the shoulder. He shook it. *Nothing.* No response.

And the man's head was turned away from him, so he couldn't tell how badly he'd been hurt. Scott shook a little harder.

Still nothing. "Come on, laddie," he said hopefully. "Wake up. I dinnae have all *day.*"

Finally, his shaking finally had an effect: it made the man's head loll around to face him. And suddenly there was no doubt in Scott's mind who this was, or why he didn't answer.

It was Chief Engineer Sachs. And half his face had been shorn away in the crash.

"My god," whispered Scotty. "My dear god."

Turning away from the spectre of death, he crept toward the base of an engineering console. Hanging onto it as best he could, he got one leg underneath him, then the other. And finally, with a gargantuan effort, he straightened up.

For an awful moment, his head swam and he felt as if he were going to be sick. The moment passed.

Unfortunately, the pain in his arm was mounting, getting worse. It felt for all the world as if it were on fire. Ignoring the terrible ache for the moment, he peered through the stinging smoke, trying to get a handle on the situation.

Suddenly, a geyser of sparks erupted from somewhere nearby, throwing the immediate vicinity into stark relief. Scott saw at least one more body— bloody, inert, lying on the deck in an impossible position.

Was he the only one who'd lived to tell the tale, then? Could his luck have been that good?

Again, the pain came washing over him, making his knees weak . . . challenging him for control of the flesh that was Montgomery Scott. But hanging onto the console, he beat it back by force of will.

And noted that the engineering station was still working. Its screen was still alive—dusted with soot from the smoke, but still functional. Wiping away a thin layer of soot with his hand, Scott called up a bioprofile of the *Jenolen*.

It wasn't good news that confronted him there. It wasn't good news at all.

Michael Jan Friedman

Besides himself, there was only one other survivor.
Scott shook his head in disbelief. Only *one?*

How could that be? Brows knit, he checked to see
that the station wasn't malfunctioning—but it passed
the diagnostic review with flying colors.

Scott massaged one of his temples with a forefinger.
Out of all those passengers and crew members . . .
only two had survived? It wasn't possible. If *he* had
come through the crash, surely the men and women
abovedecks, in their nice, secure turbulence-berths,
should have fared even better.

They *had* to be alive. They had to—

And then he saw it: a flashing light in the screen's
hull-integrity field. Scott moaned in sympathy.

That's why the others hadn't made it. The impact
had created a tiny rupture in the hull—probably no
larger than his palm, but big enough to suck out all the
air on the passenger deck.

The force of the crash hadn't killed them. They'd
bloody well *suffocated.*

Scott wanted to cry out. He wanted to howl at the
injustice of it, at the loss of life.

But it wasn't the first time he'd wanted to do that.
Like all the other times, he bit his lip and went on.

There was another survivor, he reminded himself,
forcing his eyes to focus on the monitor again. Somewhere in all this charred ruin, there was a life that
could still be preserved. And the man was lying
somewhere nearby—not more than a few meters
away, he judged from the floorplan.

Then, as if to confirm that the internal sensors knew
what they were talking about, there was movement
amid the drifts of smoke. A shape, dark and stum-

28

bling. A familiar profile, glistening wet with blood in the spark-shot chaos.

"Franklin!" called Scott. His voice was a harsh rasp—but it did the trick. It got the ensign's attention. "Over here, lad!"

The younger man's head turned. His eyes glittered wildly, reflecting the fireworks spewing out of a caved-in console. And he said something, though Scott couldn't quite make it out.

"I cannae hear ye!" he croaked.

Franklin lurched forward until he could grab the older man's shoulder. His head bleeding from a gash in his forehead, he leaned close and said: "They're *dead,* sir. They're all *dead.*"

Scott gripped the hand that held his shoulder and met the ensign's horror-stricken gaze. "I know, lad, I know. But *we're* still alive. And if we want to stay that way, we've got to make some sense out o' this mess."

Franklin nodded. Taking a deep breath, he regained control of himself. "All right," he said at last, his voice still trembling a bit, but stronger than before. "I'm with you, sir."

"Good lad. Now then . . ." Punching up the ship's diagnostic systems, Scott considered the damage. No welcome news here either. The crash had disabled everything except auxiliary life support and communications—and those systems might go down before long as well. Just as bad, the ship's supplies of food and drink had been contaminated by radiation leaking from the now-irreparable impulse engines.

"It doesn't look promising," observed the ensign, "does it?"

Scott shook his head. "No, laddie, it does nae. Even

if the auxiliary power batteries keep it livable in here, we've got nothing to eat or drink. We can still call for help, but it may be a long time in coming."

He could see Franklin's Adam's apple crawl the length of his throat. Nor could he blame the man. They were doomed—just as surely as if they'd perished in the collision with the sphere along with the others.

Unless . . .

Scott peered through the smoke in the direction of the transporter platform. "On the other hand," he told Franklin, "we may still have a card or two to play before we're done."

"Captain Scott . . . ?" said the ensign.

"Send a distress signal," the older man instructed. "Code one alpha zero."

Before Franklin could reply, Scott was on his way to the transporter station, feeling his way through the smoke from console to console. With each halting step, he worked out another detail of what had started out as only a kernel of an idea.

"Let's see," he muttered. "I'll need a way to keep the signal from degrading. And a power source . . ."

A moment later, he found the transporter station. Fortunately, it hadn't suffered so much as a scratch. It was as if someone was looking out for them, seeing to it that they had at least a fighting chance to buck the odds.

After all, neither he nor Franklin should have been in the Ops center when the Dyson Sphere was discovered. They should have been in the passenger section, Scott perusing *The Laws of Physics* for the umpteenth time, Franklin doing whatever it was he did when he was off-duty.

But Scott hadn't been able to resist looking at the problem with the warp drive. And when it became apparent that the *Jenolen* was going to crash, he'd stubbornly decided to stick it out in the Ops center. If he hadn't been first curious and then foolish, he and his young friend would have perished by now—suffocating along with the others when the air rushed out of the passenger deck.

Luck? Kismet? Blind Fortune? Scott cursed softly. Men make their own luck, his grandfather Clifford had once told him. And his grandfather was right, he mused, as he set to work prying the circuit panel off the back of the transporter station with his good arm.

"I've sent the signal," the ensign announced from the other end of the Ops center. "Maximum range, continuous loop."

"Good man," answered Scott. "Now get yourself over to the transporter controls. I can use some help."

He'd no sooner said that than the panel came free of its berth, exposing the innards of the console. Though the only light he had available was that of a flaming control panel somewhere behind him, Scott popped out the tiny tool on the inside of the panel and set to work on the diagnostic circuitry.

Fortunately, things hadn't changed much. In fact, in some ways, the *Jenolen*'s transporter technology was inferior to that of the *Enterprise*. But then the *Jenolen* was only a transport vessel and the *Enterprise* had been the flagship of the fleet.

"Captain Scott?" said a voice.

He jumped at the nearness of it, then realized it was only Franklin. "Dinnae sneak up on me that way, lad. There's enough here to make me jumpy without *you* spookin' me into the bargain!"

The ensign looked contrite. "Sorry, sir." He held up what looked like a long piece of velour. A somehow *familiar*-looking piece of velour. "Judging from the way you're holding your arm, I thought you might be more comfortable in *this.*"

Abruptly, Scott understood. "A sling," he said out loud. Not a bad idea, either. If his arm was hurt half as badly as it felt, it would be good to keep it immobile. "Where did ye get it?" he asked.

Franklin held up his right forearm, showing the older man a ragged sleeve that now ended at the elbow. "I figured you needed it more than I did," he said, draping the strip of material around Scott's neck and tying the ends together underneath his injured limb.

Scott tested it. Not bad, not bad at all. He could move around now a good deal more easily. He looked at the ensign, intending to express his thanks.

But before he could get a word out, Franklin tilted his head toward the open transporter unit. "You said you needed help, sir?"

"Aye," Scott acknowledged. There would be time enough for thanks later. "Here's what I'd like ye to do. Y'see these circuits? They enable the transporter's diagnostic function." He used the tool to point to a spot where they nearly converged, then handed the tool to Franklin. "Take this and meld the circuits."

The ensign's soot-blackened forehead furrowed

right down the middle. "But won't that lock the pattern buffer into a diagnostic cycle?"

Scott smiled approvingly. "Aye, lad. It'll keep the signal cycling in a perpetual diagnostic mode."

Franklin looked at him. "But why?"

"Ye'll see," the older man told him, "as soon as I've made a few adjustments of my own." And with that, Scott got to his feet.

The smoke was starting to clear a bit—a good sign that life support was working as well as the monitors said. But with any luck, Scott thought, they wouldn't have to worry about that too much longer.

Concentrating on the control panel, he called up a diagram of its link to the auxiliary power batteries. Unfortunately, it wouldn't supply enough juice for what he had in mind.

Frowning, Scott brought up a second diagram— that of the emitter array. As he'd hoped, it was as intact as the rest of the transporter assembly.

One more diagram—a cross section of the phase inducers. He nodded, satisfied. No damage there either. So far so good.

Now came the iffy part, the part he wasn't entirely confident about. After all, the phase inducers weren't meant to work with the emitter array. That's not what their designers had in mind.

Of course, their designers had never been in a wrecked transport with starvation and slow death looking them in the eye. Holding his breath, Scott asked the computer to cross-connect the inducers to the array.

If it worked, they'd have a regenerating power

source—one that could keep the transporter running until help arrived. If it didn't, they'd be back to square one.

It *worked*.

"Damn," Scott breathed, consumed by a wave of relief.

"Everything all right up there?" asked Franklin.

"Everything's fine," said the older man. "Just fine, laddie. And down there?"

"Almost done," the ensign told him. "There." Rolling back onto his haunches, Franklin popped the tool into the back of the panel and then put the panel back where it belonged.

As if neatness counted. Scott couldn't help but chuckle, even under these most macabre of circumstances.

The ensign stood. "Now what, sir?"

The older man pointed to the transporter platform. "Now we go for a long ride, laddie. Though if our luck continues to hold, maybe it will nae be *too* long."

Franklin didn't get it. "Where are we going?" he asked. "If our sensors can't penetrate the sphere, there's no way we can *beam* inside. And even if we could, we don't know what it's like in there. It could be . . ." His voice trailed off as realization dawned. "Wait a minute. With the pattern buffer locked into a diagnostic cycle, we can't go *anywhere*. Our atoms will just keep . . . flowing through it. Over and over and over again."

Scott nodded. "That's exactly right. Over and over again—until someone answers our distress call and brings us out of it."

The ensign shook his head in admiration. "How did you ever think of that?"

"Laddie," said Scott, "it's my job to think of that. Or at least it used to be." He indicated the platform again. "Shall we?"

Franklin hesitated. "What . . . what if it doesn't work?"

Scott shrugged. "Then we'll be nae worse off than if we'd sat around waiting for it. And maybe better, depending on how ye look at it."

That seemed to make sense to the younger man. Anyway, he didn't ask any more questions. He just made his way to the transporter platform and took his place on one of the two positions there.

Brave lad, Scott thought. Reminds me of myself when I was a wee bit younger. No . . . make that a *lot* younger.

In any case, time was a-wastin'. Working the controls one last time, Scott set the mechanism for a thirty-second delay and activated it. Then he took the dozen or so steps necessary to ascend the platform.

As he took his place, Scott surveyed the carnage all around them . . . the charred bulkheads, the still-sparking control panels, the burning bodies of the two poor souls who hadn't made it the way they had. If he and Franklin could come through *that,* they could come through *anything*.

Franklin turned to him. "See you on the other side," he said, managing a smile.

"Aye, lad," said Scott. "On the other side."

Chapter One

USS Enterprise 1701-D
Seventy-five years later

AT THE SOUND OF his door chimes, Captain Jean-Luc Picard looked up from his monitor, where he'd been reviewing a monograph on accretion bridges in binary star pairs. Touching the appropriate panel on his control padd, he stored the file.

"Come," said Picard, triggering the entry mechanism.

As the door slid aside, it revealed the visitor the captain had been expecting. He gestured to the seat opposite him.

"Won't you have a seat, Mr. Kane?"

Ensign Darrin Kane was a tall, athletic-looking young man with reddish hair, piercing eyes and a ready smile. At least, that was how he'd appeared to Picard in the past. Right now, the ensign looked all too serious, almost sullen.

"Thank you, sir," said Kane, pulling out the chair and seating himself.

The captain leaned back. "How is your father, Ensign?"

Kane smiled, but the expression didn't seem to come very easily to him. "He's fine, sir. I heard from him just the other day via subspace packet. He's been riding, golfing, hiking . . . you name it. He says he should have quit Starfleet a long time ago."

Picard chuckled. "Indeed. The Ferris Kane *I* knew couldn't have been pried loose from his captain's chair with a crowbar. But then, people change, don't they? I suppose the day will come when I'll prefer the good life to Starfleet as well."

Privately, he couldn't imagine such a day—not even in his wildest dreams. But it wouldn't have been polite to tell young Kane that, after his father had opted for a carefree civilian life back on Earth.

"So," said the captain, "what prompted this meeting? You made it sound as if it were rather urgent."

The ensign bit his lip. For a second or two, he seemed to hesitate. Then, suddenly, he got to his feet.

"I'm sorry, sir. I shouldn't be wasting your time with this sort of thing. Just forget I ever came to see you . . . please." And with that, he turned to walk out.

"Ensign Kane?" said Picard, his voice ringing out a little louder than he'd intended. But after all, his curiosity had been piqued. He wasn't about to let this mystery go on any longer.

Kane stopped in his tracks and looked back at the captain. "Sir?"

"Sit," Picard commanded.

Again, the ensign hesitated.

"That's an order, Mr. Kane."

Looking just a bit like a cornered animal, he sat. But it was a while before he raised his eyes to return the captain's gaze.

"Now then," said Picard, "you came to see me for a reason. Mind you, I will not force that reason out of you. It's ultimately your choice as to whether or not you'd like to talk about it. But I *would* like to hear it."

The ensign sighed. "All right, sir." His temples worked. "It has to do with Commander Riker."

Will? That was a surprise. "What about Commander Riker?" the captain prodded.

Kane cleared his throat. "I believe . . . he has something against me, sir. He seems to be harboring a certain . . . I don't know. *Resentment.*"

That didn't sound like Will Riker, thought Picard. "And how has this resentment manifested itself?" he asked.

The younger man sighed. "Sir, I graduated from the Academy at the top of my class. That wasn't because I was the brightest or most talented cadet there. It was because I *wanted* it more than anyone else."

"I am well aware of your accomplishments at the Academy," the captain interjected, hoping to keep the conversation on a lighter note.

"Please, sir . . . let me finish. When I was assigned to the *Hornet,* I didn't rest on my laurels. I worked hard—harder than any other ensign aboard. Captain Peterson will attest to that."

Again, something of which Picard had full knowledge. But he didn't wish to interrupt a second time.

"When I was transferred to the *Enterprise,* it was like a dream come true. My father had always spoken very highly of you, sir. And also of your ship. I told myself that all my hard work had paid off. But I also knew that the hardest work was still ahead."

A pause. "But?" said the captain.

"But I haven't been given a *chance* here. I'm willing to put in the hours. I'm willing to accept responsibility. I'm willing to do whatever it takes to become a captain myself one day. But I'm not going to get there by checking cargo day in and day out."

"Cargo oversight *is* one of the duties assigned to ensigns on this ship," Picard reminded him.

"I understand that, sir. And I wouldn't mind doing it—if I also got the opportunity to do something *more*. Or, for that matter, if I was only being treated the same as everyone else. Out of all the ensigns on the *Enterprise*, I'm the only one who hasn't even gotten near the bridge level—until now. And with all due respect, Captain, your ready room isn't quite the part of the bridge I had in mind."

Picard nodded. "Have you discussed this with Commander Riker himself, Ensign?"

"Yes, sir," Kane replied. "On more than one occasion. And he's told me that the assignments he gives his ensigns are his own business—not a matter that's open to discussion."

"I see," said the captain. He considered the ensign and could see no hint of duplicity in him. He appeared to be telling the truth.

But if that were so, then Riker was guilty of some sort of private vendetta. And that didn't seem very likely.

Abruptly, Kane got to his feet again. "I didn't mean

to take up so much of the captain's time," he remarked.

"Don't apologize," Picard told him. He stood as well. "You can be sure I will look into the situation, Ensign."

Kane looked grateful. "That's all I ask, sir."

Lt. Commander Data had come a long way toward understanding human beings in the handful of years he'd served aboard the *Enterprise*. And one of the human beings he had come to understand best was his commanding officer, Captain Picard.

Data had barely joined the crew of the *Enterprise* when he noticed that Picard was given to extensive use of his ready room. It was a matter of style; some captains preferred to spend most of their time in their command seats, while others sat there only when it was absolutely necessary. Picard leaned more toward the latter than the former.

But even among those who retreated to their sanctums at the drop of a communicator, there were stylistic differences. Some wished to be left alone as much as possible; others wanted to be alerted to every little detail of the ship's management, no matter how slight or inconsequential.

On this behavioral axis, Picard favored the former more than the latter. Nor was it a matter of reclusiveness, as the android had suspected early on. The captain simply felt that once he had selected the best people for the job, they should be allowed to do that job.

By the same token, he did not expect to be interrupted needlessly. After all, a ship's captain had a job to do as well, and much of it—too much, some would say—came in the form of correspondence, analysis and continuing education.

Unfortunately for Data, he'd had to learn Picard's foibles the hard way. In his first day on the bridge, he had found occasion to invade the sanctity of the captain's ready room half a dozen times—until Picard finally called him in for a one-on-one meeting.

"Mr. Data," he'd said, his voice thick with what the android now recognized as irony, "have you never heard of something called *initiative?* Do you intend to check with me before *breathing?"*

Data's answer had been: "Of course not, sir. Breathing is an involuntary part of my program. The process requires no conscious decisions. However, if it ever becomes preferable *not* to breathe . . ."

"You will make that choice on your *own,"* the captain had finished, in a carefully measured tone. He'd studied the android for a moment. "Data, if I wanted to make all the decisions myself—or thought I needed to—I'd be out there on the bridge twenty-four hours a day. You were selected to be this ship's second officer because you are *good* at what you do. Because I *trust* you to be my surrogate. Is that clear?"

Data had nodded. "Quite clear, sir."

And ever since that juncture, he had made it his business to take care of all matters within his purview —leaving only the most important judgments to Captain Picard. Nor had the captain ever found it necessary to have that discussion with him again.

So it was that when Data discovered something unexpected in a routine sensor sweep, he initially made no mention of it to the captain. First, he isolated it. Then he recorded it. Then he verified that it was precisely what it seemed to be. And finally, he analyzed it.

Only then, when he was sure that he had come across something of genuine interest, did he decide it would be best to alert his commanding officer.

Darrin Kane was riding high. Higher, in fact, than Andy Sousa had ever seen him.

"I knew I could get somewhere if I talked to the captain," said Kane. "I knew he'd bring that spit-and-polish sonuvagun Riker down a peg."

Sousa found it hard to believe that a word or two from his fellow ensign had been enough to sway the captain. From what he'd seen, Picard wasn't a man easily bamboozled.

"Are you sure he *did* bring him down a peg?"

Kane nodded. "Damned sure. The captain and my old man are buddies from way back. As far as Picard knows, I'm a real golden boy, a chip off the old block. There's no way he's going to let that bearded wonder off the hook."

As they negotiated a bend in the corridor, a pair of female civilians passed them going in the other direction. Kane flashed a grin at them; they grinned back.

Sousa wished he could do that. He wished he could be that confident, that sure of himself. It just wasn't in his makeup.

That's why Kane would probably be a captain before his thirtieth birthday, and Sousa would be lucky to be a captain at all. *Ever.*

Sure, he'd made a good start here on the *Enterprise*.

He was well-liked, even praised from time to time for his work at the conn. But as Kane had told him on more than one occasion, nice guys finished last—if they finished at all.

"Hey, helm-jockey. I think this is your stop."

"Huh?"

Sousa turned to see that he'd left his fellow ensign behind, standing next to the turbolift. He'd been so lost in thought that he'd forgotten where he was going.

"This *is* where you wanted to go, isn't it?" Kane grinned. "Or have you discovered some kind of secret passage up to the bridge?"

"Very funny," said Sousa. Feeling his cheeks grow hot, he avoided the other man's gaze as he headed for the lift.

"See you in the rec after hours, helm-jockey. I'll be the one with the big smile on his face," Kane told him.

As the doors to the lift opened, Sousa turned back to look at his companion. "Yeah," he said. "See you in the rec."

Then the doors closed and Sousa was on his way up to the bridge, wishing he'd been cut from the same cloth as Darrin Kane.

"Captain Picard?"

Picard was still pondering Ensign Kane's situation when he heard the android's voice come in over the intercom. "Yes, Data?"

"Sir, there is something here you should see."

The captain nodded. "I'm on my way."

Rising, he rounded his desk and headed for the exit. Kane's problem would have to wait. Mr. Data would not have summoned him unless this were a matter of some urgency.

As the ready room doors slid aside, he noted that the turbolift doors were parting as well. And as Picard crossed to Data's position at the aft science station, the lift discharged two figures: his first officer and Ensign Sousa, both of whom were due to begin their shifts.

With a glance at the captain, Riker saw that something was up. "Sir?" he said.

Picard didn't answer. He merely gestured for Riker to join him. With the two of them converging on the science station, the android turned to look over his shoulder at them.

"What is it, Data?" asked Picard.

"A subspace radio wave," came the reply. As the captain and his first officer bent over the station's monitor array, Data expanded on the statement. "I have identified the signal. The transmission appears to be a Starfleet code used between fifty and eighty years ago." Working at the console a moment longer, he paused. "Code one alpha zero. Ship in distress."

From force of habit, Riker looked up at the intercom grid. Not that it was at all necessary; the computer would have picked up his voice just as clearly if he'd faced the deck instead—or for that matter, spoken in a whisper. "Computer, are there any Starfleet vessels reported missing in this sector?"

The computer's response was prompt and succinct. "Negative."

Picard cleared his throat before he amended the computer's directive. "Expand parameters to include adjacent sectors."

A list of ships came up on one of the monitors. Again, the audible response was almost instantaneous. "Transport ship SS *Jenolen,* NC five-six-seven, was reported missing on stardate seven-eight-nine-three-point-one while en route to Norpin Five."

Riker frowned. "Seventy-five years ago. I'd say we've found the *Jenolen*—but we're a long way from Norpin Five. They must've gone pretty far off course."

Picard nodded. "Indeed."

He turned to Sousa, who was sitting at the conn station. Sousa peered out at him from under his shock of dark, unruly hair.

"Ensign, establish coordinates for the source of the signal and plot a course for them. Warp factor eight."

"Aye, sir," answered Sousa, getting to work.

Riker looked at the captain. "Warp factor eight?" he repeated in a low voice, so that only he, Data and Picard could hear it. "Why the hurry?"

The captain frowned. His first officer had a point. If the *Jenolen* had been waiting for seventy-five years, it could wait a little longer. It wasn't as if there were going to be any survivors at this late juncture.

And yet . . .

Picard shrugged. "Call it intuition," he said, and left it at that.

Chapter Two

WILL RIKER drummed his fingers on the armrest of his seat in the command center. Stealing a glance at the stony visage of Captain Picard, who was again standing beside Data at the aft science station, he tried for the umpteenth time to decide if it was his imagination . . . or if the captain was, for some reason, avoiding him.

For four days, they'd been riding the currents of that bizarre reality known as subspace, heading for a rendezvous with what was left of the *Jenolen*. And in all that time, Picard hadn't met his first officer's gaze.

For a long time, it had been just a nagging suspicion. Now, Riker was almost certain of it . . . even tempted to confront the captain with his observations.

No. He reigned himself in. If Picard wanted to discuss the matter—whatever it was—he would do so

47

in his own good time. And that was his right. He
would do as he thought best.

Maybe after the *Jenolen* had been discovered and
explored, Picard would put his cards on the table.
Yes . . . that's it, Riker decided. He wants to devote
all his attention to the *Jenolen*. And when that's over,
he'll take me aside and tell me what's on his mind.

"Captain?" It was Worf.

Turning away from the science console, Picard
answered him. "Yes, Lieutenant?"

"We are approaching the coordinates of the distress
signal," the Klingon reported.

No surprise there. All it meant was that they were
right on schedule.

Nonetheless, Picard nodded his acknowledgment of
the fact. Turning to Rager, he said: "Bring us out of
warp, Ensign Rager. All stop."

Rager, a spritelike black woman, complied. "Aye,
sir. All stop."

Riker stood, tired of keeping his seat. He got antsy
whenever the ship was about to close in on its
objective—particularly one it had been pursuing as
long as this one.

Though the main viewscreen showed nothing except an unfamiliar starfield, he found himself straining to see anything that vaguely resembled a transport
vessel. Needless to say, he had no success. They were
still millions of kilometers short of the signal's source,
which they would now approach on impulse power.

He'd barely finished his thought when the *Enterprise* was rocked—as if a giant hand had grasped it
and was shaking it like a tambourine. Riker grasped at

the back of Rager's chair to keep from being catapulted across the deck.

Then, as suddenly as it had started, the shaking stopped. But that was no guarantee that they wouldn't be treated to a repeat performance.

"Yellow alert," cried Riker, his voice reverberating throughout the enclosed space and spreading to the rest of the ship via the intercom system.

At the same time, he headed back to his place in the command center. Picard and Data were less than a step behind him, moving toward their own customary positions on the bridge.

"Report," intoned Picard, as he took his seat a little uncertainly.

"We have entered a massive gravitational field," replied Worf.

Picard turned to look at him. He wasn't alone. After all, there was nothing on the screen *close* enough to possess a gravitational field—much less one as powerful as the one they'd run into.

"Mr. Data?" the captain said, hoping for more information.

The android was bent over the Ops station, where he'd replaced the crewman who had been sitting there before. "There are no stars or other stellar bodies listed at these coordinates on our navigational charts." He paused. "However, sensor readings indicate the presence of an extremely strong gravitational source in this vicinity." Another pause. "Directly ahead."

It didn't make sense, Riker told himself. Unless . . . the object creating the field was cloaked somehow.

Picard must have had the same idea. "Mr. Worf," he said, "can you localize the source of the gravity field?"

For a moment, the Klingon worked at his console. Then he looked up. "Yes, sir."

Good, thought the first officer. Now we're getting somewhere.

"On screen," said the captain.

The starfield on the viewscreen changed, reflecting another view. And if one looked closely, there was a small, dark ball at its center.

"Magnify," commanded Picard.

The image jumped up several orders of magnitude, until the dark ball could be seen more easily. After the final jump, it appeared as round and smooth as a billiard ball—but because it was so dark, it was hard to discern anything else about it.

It mystified Riker. He'd never seen anything like it.

"Sensors?" he said, finally breaking the spell. They needed information—and they needed it as quickly as possible. Who knew what other surprises awaited them in this gravitational field?

"I am having difficulty scanning the object," said Data. "However, it would appear to be at least two hundred million kilometers in diameter."

Riker looked to Picard. The captain's surprise mirrored his own.

"That's almost the size of Earth's orbit around the sun," the first officer blurted.

"Indeed," said Picard. "Why didn't we detect it before now?"

Data swiveled in his chair to face him. "The object's enormous mass is causing a great deal of gravimetric subspace interference. That interference might have prevented our sensors from detecting the object before we dropped out of warp."

There was a beat as they all looked up at this strange object on the screen. Suddenly, a look of wonder came across Picard's face. He might have found something hitherto only imagined.

"Mr. Data," said Picard, "could this be a . . . a Dyson Sphere?"

Data seemed to ponder the information. "There is no comparative data, Captain. However, this object does fit the general parameters of Dyson's theory."

Riker looked from one of them to the other. "A Dyson Sphere?" he echoed.

Picard nodded. "It's a very old theory, Number One. I'm not surprised you haven't heard of it." Turning again to the viewscreen, he regarded the dark ball. "A twentieth-century physicist, Freeman Dyson, postulated that an enormous hollow sphere could be constructed around a star. This would have the advantage of harnessing *all* the radiant energy of the star, not just a tiny fraction of it. A population living on the interior surface would therefore have a virtually inexhaustible source of power."

Riker's eyes narrowed. "Are you saying there might be people living in there?" he asked the captain.

The answer was supplied by Data. "Possibly a great number of people, Commander. The interior surface area of a sphere this size would be equivalent to that of more than two hundred fifty *million* class-M planets."

Hard to believe, Riker told himself. He tried to picture a civilization thriving on the inside skin of the sphere. Hell, the horizon would curve up instead of down. And . . .

His mind recoiled at the image. He'd seen his share of strange phenomena as first officer of the *Enterprise*, but none of them had prepared him for something like this.

Worf spoke up from his position behind the Tactical console. "Sir . . . I have located the distress signal. It is coming from a point on the northern hemisphere."

Absorbing the information, Picard turned to the ensign at the conn. "Ensign Rager, take us into synchronous orbit above that point."

"Aye, sir," said Rager, her fingers fairly flying over her controls.

They still had to answer the seventy-five-year-old distress call, Riker mused. But their interest in the *Jenolen* had already paled beside their interest in the sphere. Gradually, they pulled closer to it. And closer still.

Before long, the monstrous object looked like a giant wall in space, stretching in every direction as far as the eye could see. Where before, the sphere had appeared perfectly smooth, it was now possible to discern intricate patterns on the surface—patterns that suggested construction supports. However, they were still too far away to make out anything distinct.

All eyes were riveted to the viewscreen. What they saw there was just too immense, too unique to miss a single detail.

At last, they achieved the synchronous orbit that Picard had desired. "We are holding position at thirty thousand kilometers above the surface," announced Sousa.

"The distress signal is coming from a Federation ship that has impacted on the surface of the sphere," said Data. After a moment, he confirmed what they had already suspected. "It is the transport ship *Jenolen,* Captain."

"Life signs?" asked Riker.

"Our sensors show none," the android responded. "However, there are several small power emanations . . . and life support is still functioning at minimum levels."

Out of the corner of his eye, Riker noticed Picard looking at him. He looked back and nodded.

"Bridge to engineering," announced the first officer. "Geordi, meet me in Transporter Room Three." Then, turning to the Klingon security chief, he said: "Mr. Worf, you're with me."

As another crew member took over at Tactical, Worf followed Riker into the turbolift. The doors had barely closed when the Klingon grunted.

"I know," said Riker. "You'd rather be studying the insides of that sphere than the insides of a derelict transport vessel." He looked up at the lift's luminous ceiling and scowled. "I don't blame you. So would I."

As Geordi materialized on the *Jenolen,* with Riker on one side of him and Worf on the other, he scanned their surroundings. Before joining his colleagues in the transporter room, he'd taken a moment to study the layout of the vessel with Chief O'Brien—mostly to make sure they didn't beam themselves into a bulkhead—so he wasn't surprised at the size or configuration of the Ops center.

However, neither the first officer nor the security

chief were quite so well prepared. "Cramped," commented Worf.

Riker nodded. "And it seems they did everything in here but cook dinner."

"Maybe that too," Geordi remarked.

Each of them took out his tricorder. "Come on," said the first officer. "Let's have a gander at the place."

The lights were dim and there didn't seem to be any equipment working at present, but that didn't present a problem to Geordi—who, thanks to his VISOR, could "see" almost as easily in the dark as in the light. Looking around, he made some mental notes.

One or two of the consoles were damaged or burnt out, there were piles of ash on the floor, and in several spots the bulkhead was caved in. "This ship really went through the ringer," he concluded, "even before it crashed. Wonder what happened to it."

Sniffing the air, Riker frowned. "Pretty stale," he observed.

Geordi consulted his tricorder. "Life support is barely operating."

Turning to Worf, the first officer said: "See if you can increase the oxygen level, Lieutenant."

Nodding, Worf moved over to one of the consoles. Meanwhile, Geordi's tricorder led him to the transporter controls. Not that he expected to find anything of interest there, but he had to cover all the bases.

A moment later, he was glad he had. "Commander," said the chief engineer, his heart beating a little faster at his discovery.

Riker moved over to see what he'd found. "What is it, Geordi?"

"The transporter is still on-line," said La Forge. "It's being fed power from the auxiliary systems."

Riker bent over the transporter controls to do some checking of his own. "How about that," he muttered. "The rematerialization subroutine has been disabled."

"And that's not all," Geordi added. "The auxiliary phase inducers have been connected to the emitter array. The override is completely gone. And the pattern buffer's been locked into a continuous diagnostic cycle."

Riker shook his head. "This doesn't make any sense. Locking the unit in a diagnostic mode just sends inert matter flowing through the pattern buffer. Why would anyone want to—?"

Suddenly, Geordi saw something on the console— something he hadn't noticed before. "Damn," he breathed. "Someone's pattern is still in the buffer!"

If his heartbeat had accelerated before, it was pounding now.

Riker scrutinized the reading. "You're right," he concluded. "It's completely intact." The first officer looked up at him, amazed. "Less than point zero zero three signal degradation. How is that possible?"

"I don't know," said Geordi, his mind racing. "I've never seen a transporter system jury-rigged like this. He turned to the monitor again, aware that Riker was doing the same.

"Could someone . . . survive in a transporter buffer for seventy-five years?" asked the first officer.

Geordi bit his lip. Was it possible? It had never been attempted . . . not to his knowledge, anyway. But . . .

"I know a way to find out," he said.

Riker looked at him. "You mean get him out? Or try to?" His brow knit. "Assuming, of course, that there's someone in there in the first place."

Geordi nodded. "Yup. That's just what I mean."

Riker thought for a second. "All right," he said. "Give it a shot."

Of course, it wouldn't be easy. It was one thing to run a twenty-fourth century transporter console, with all its automatic settings and its sophisticated backup systems—and quite another to try to salvage an ancient signal from a makeshift loop using yesterday's technology.

For instance, he didn't dare disconnect the phase inducers from the emitter array. Even though he could probably draw more power at this point from the auxiliary battery, the switch-over would leave the pattern buffer without juice for a split second—and that might be time enough for the signal to degenerate.

No, he would let the present connection stand—and just bypass the melded circuits that had turned the diagnostic function into a continuous cycle. Then it would just be a matter of re-enabling the rematerialization subroutine and . . . if he was lucky . . . *presto* . . . one very weary transporter-traveler.

Ever so carefully, Geordi carried out his plan. The first part went as smooth as silk. The second, not so smooth.

"What's the matter?" asked Riker, seeing the look on the engineer's face.

Geordi shook his head. "The subroutine that governs rematerialization. It doesn't seem to want to come back."

The first officer grunted. "Don't give it a choice."

"I won't," Geordi agreed. This time, he took a different tack—and broke out into a grin.

"You got it?" Riker guessed.

"I got it."

Only one thing left to do now, Geordi mused. Activating a final control, he looked to the tiny transporter platform.

In the next instant, he saw the beginnings of an old-fashioned transporter effect—both less stable and less spectacular than the one with which he was familiar. Inwardly, he cheered the unit on.

Come on, damn it. Work—just one more time. Spit this guy out.

At last, a figure took shape. It wavered in the beam, taking on density at a snail's pace, until Geordi wasn't sure it would ever materialize completely. Then, with a last surge of energy, the shape became a man.

"My god," said Riker. "You did it."

And so he had. For what stood before them was a living, breathing denizen of the twenty-third century. And except for the arm he held in a sling, he was hardly the worse for wear.

Chapter Three

FOR A MOMENT OR TWO, Scott was overcome by a wave of vertigo. He didn't know who he was, much less where he was. His arm was in a sling, though he didn't remember how it had gotten that way. Then his reeling senses started to steady themselves and it all came flooding back to him.

He was in the *Jenolen*—in the Ops center. They'd crashed. Only he and Ensign Franklin had survived. And with a dearth of supplies staring them in the face, their only hope had been . . .

He looked around. There were two men standing in front of the transporter platform, looking at him. Staring, actually. One of them, the shorter of the two, wore a strange high-tech band around his eyes. Both sported uniforms that he'd never seen before. But they were blessedly human and neither of them seemed to pose a threat to him.

Besides which, they'd rescued him from the transporter loop. So how bad could they possibly be?

The transporter loop, he thought. *Franklin.* Where was Franklin?

Shaking off his wooziness, Scott came down off the platform and headed straight for the transporter control console. As he passed his rescuers, he graced them with a single nod.

"Thank ye, lads," he said.

Seemingly fascinated by him, they stepped aside to let him bustle by. No sooner had Scott reached the console than he began checking out its monitors . . . verifying his readings . . .

"We've got to get Franklin out of there," he said, more to himself than to either of the two onlookers.

"Someone else's pattern is still in the buffer?" asked the one with the high-tech band. There was a note of genuine concern in his voice.

"Aye," Scott said absently. "Matt Franklin and I went in together."

Almost done, he told himself. Another couple of levels to examine. Here . . . and here . . . and then he'd . . .

Wait a minute. Scott stared at the last monitor, the one that covered the inducers. He didn't like this. He didn't like this one wee bit.

"Something's wrong," he said out loud, hearing the strain of panic in his voice. "One of the inducers has failed . . ." Turning to the man in the band, he barked: "Boost the gain on the matter stream."

The man complied, apparently unhampered by the thing on his face. Moving to a nearby console, he carried out Scott's instructions.

"Come on, Franklin," he breathed, trying to dredge up more information. As long as the lad's signal pattern was unaffected, he could bypass the bad inducer and bring him back through one of the good ones. "Don't give up, Matt. I *know* you're in there. I can hear your *electrons* buzzin' . . ."

Scott's mouth had gone dry, so dry he could barely swallow. He worked furiously at his instruments, certain that he could perform one more miracle. After all, he'd pulled Jim Kirk's bacon out of worse fires. What made this any different?

And then he saw it, flashing on one of the screens in a graphic so bright it made his eyes hurt. Franklin's signal profile.

No, he thought. Oh lord, *no*.

For a time, he didn't know how long exactly, he was transfixed. When he tore his eyes from the graphic at last, they were moist with sorrow.

The two who'd rescued him just stood there, not saying a word. After all, they hadn't known Matt Franklin. Only he had.

Still, it seemed that someone had to say it. And since it was his friend . . .

"It's no use. The signal pattern's been degraded by fifty-three percent," Scott whispered, unable to muster anything louder. "He's gone."

Despite the lack of force with which they were uttered, the last two words seemed to reverberate through the Ops center. The man wearing the band frowned and looked away.

"I'm sorry," said the other man, the taller one. He had the look of an officer who'd lost men himself. He seemed to know how it felt.

Wearily, Scott dragged his hand across his face. "So am I," he said. "He was a good lad. A brave lad. They dinnae come any better."

After a beat, the taller man moved forward. "I'm Commander William Riker," he said. "First officer of the Starship *Enterprise.*"

At the name, Scott felt something rise within him. A gladness that, just for a second or two, made him forget his sorrow.

"The *Enterprise,* eh? I should've known, lad. And I'll bet it was Kirk himself who hauled the old girl out of mothballs to come looking for me."

He took Riker's hand and shook it vigorously, wondering just when Starfleet had started outfitting its officers in these tight suits. There was barely enough room in them to hide a wart.

"Captain Montgomery Scott. How long have I been missing?"

Riker looked at his companion. The man wearing the band just shrugged.

"Well," said the first officer, "this may come as something of a shock, sir, but it's been a good . . ."

"Sir?"

The word had been spoken by someone with a deep voice. A *very* deep voice.

Scott, like the others, turned in response . . . and found himself staring at a savage, bony-browed Klingon, the same kind of villain who'd tried to take his life time and again during his exploits under Jim Kirk.

A Klingon . . . not attacking them, not even spitting in rage at them. Just standing there as casual as you please.

And, impossible as it seemed, the bloody heathen was wearing the same kind of uniform as Commander Riker. Did that mean . . . could it *possibly* mean . . . ?

But how could that be? It was one thing to sign a treaty with the barbarians . . . but this! Scott felt himself getting light-headed.

Unlike the human, however, the Klingon seemed unperturbed. Turning to the first officer, he said: "I have restored life support. The oxygen levels will return to normal shortly." Then, finally noticing the intensity with which Scott was scrutinizing him, Worf returned the stare.

"Captain Scott?"

He turned and saw Riker looking down at him. The man seemed . . . sympathetic.

"Aye?" Scott got out.

"This is Lieutenant Worf," Riker told him.

"Lieutenant?" Scott muttered. He'd been hoping there was some other explanation.

Worf's eyes narrowed ever so slightly. "Yes. *Lieutenant.*"

Scott continued to stare at him . . . until Riker moved to his side. Gently, the first officer said: "Captain Scott . . . perhaps there are a few things we should talk about."

Scott turned to him, feeling very much up the stream without a paddle. "Aye, laddie. Perhaps *more* than a few."

It took a while for them to brief him on the truth. And a lot longer before he could even come close to accepting it.

My god, thought Scott. Seventy-five years. *Seventy-five years . . .*

Transporter Chief Miles O'Brien wasn't quite sure he'd heard right. "Would you repeat that, Commander?"

"Four to beam up," Riker confirmed.

O'Brien shrugged. Was this some kind of macabre joke? That transport vessel had crashed seventy-five years ago.

"Oh, well," he said out loud. "Mine is not to reason why."

Opening up the scope of his annular confinement beam, he focused it on the away team's communicator signals, confident that they would have placed their "mystery guest" in their midst. Then, satisfied that he had a good fix on them, he activated the emitter array.

A moment later, the group took shape on the platform in front of him. And sure enough, there were four of them—not just Riker, Worf and Geordi, but an older man with graying hair and a dark moustache. It wasn't until the three officers started descending from the platform that O'Brien realized the man's arm was in a makeshift sling.

But who was he? And what the devil was he doing on the *Jenolen?*

Ah, well, thought O'Brien. He supposed he'd find out about the mystery man soon enough. After all, news traveled quickly on the *Enterprise.*

When one beamed up to a starship like the *Enterprise,* it was customary to step down off the transporter platform as soon as one had materialized. There was simply no reason to linger there.

So when Geordi saw the familiar sight of Miles O'Brien behind the control console, he just naturally headed for the exit. It wasn't until he was halfway across the room that he realized they'd left their friend Captain Scott behind.

The man looked for all his advanced years like a kid in a new and unimagined candy shop, fascinated by everything he saw around him. After a moment or two, his gaze fastened itself on the overhead transporter elements.

Riker and Worf hadn't noticed that Scott wasn't with them. They were halfway to the door, and Riker was saying: "We should probably get you to sickbay. Dr. Crusher will be able to . . ."

Abruptly, he stopped and turned around. Scott was pointing up at something. He seemed to be counting. Riker's eyes met Geordi's; Geordi shrugged.

"Ye've changed the resonator array," said Scott in a barely audible voice. He wasn't addressing anyone, just thinking out loud. "Only three phase inverters."

Geordi saw the first officer turn to him. Riker was smiling. "Mr. La Forge, I think our guest is going to have a lot of engineering questions."

Geordi nodded in agreement. "Don't worry," he said. "I'll take care of him, sir."

Glancing at Scott one last time, Riker gestured for Worf to accompany him. Together, the two officers exited the transporter room. Meanwhile, Scott had moved off and was scrutinizing the bank of optical data chips set into the wall.

"Captain Scott . . . ?" Geordi ventured.

Suddenly, the older man's eyes—still focused on the machinery above him—took on an almost horrified cast. "Of all the . . . what have ye done to the duotronic enhancers?"

"Those were replaced with isolinear chips about forty years ago," Geordi explained, as inoffensively as he could.

Scott looked at him. "Isolinear chips?"

The younger man nodded.

"Forty years ago, ye say?"

He nodded again. "That's right. It's a lot more efficient now."

Scott whistled. "Aye. I'm sure o' that."

Gesturing to the exit, Geordi said: "Shall we?"

Still a little dazed, Scott replied: "Sure. Why not?"

As they passed the transporter console, O'Brien jerked a thumb in the newcomer's direction and raised his eyebrows in a question. But Geordi just smiled.

There was no explaining Scott's situation in a word or two. Maybe later, after the *Jenolen's* sole survivor had been tended to and made comfortable.

A moment later, they were in the corridor outside, headed in the direction of the nearest turbolift. Here too, Scott's eyes scanned everything in sight. He was consumed by curiosity—pretty much as Geordi would have been if he'd suddenly turned up on a twenty-fifth-century version of the *Enterprise*.

"You were saying," the younger man interjected, "that you were on your way to the Norpin Five colony when you had a warp engine failure."

"That's right," Scott confirmed. "We had an overload in one of the plasma transfer conduits. The captain brought us out of warp . . . we hit some gravimetric interference and then there it was, as big as life . . ." Pointing to a raised portion of the bulkhead, he asked: "Is that a conduit interface?"

Geordi nodded. "Yup. Uh, there it was . . . the Dyson Sphere, right?"

"Aye. It was amazing . . . an actual Dyson Sphere. Can ye imagine the engineering skills needed to even design such a structure?"

But his attention wasn't on his recollections of the sphere. It was on a wall panel a couple of meters up ahead. Suddenly, he moved up to it and pulled the panel off its place in the bulkhead.

Geordi was a little concerned—uncertain that Scott knew what he was doing. But out of courtesy, he didn't make a move to stop him.

"Liquid state energy transfer," observed the older man. "No power lines at all. This looks like an optical data conduit."

"Uh, be careful there," warned Geordi. "That's no data conduit. It's an EPS power tap."

Gently wresting the panel from Scott, he replaced it on the wall. "Tell me more about the Dyson Sphere. What happened when you first approached it?"

Scott shrugged. Up ahead, the turbolift was coming into view.

"We began a standard survey of the surface, of course. We were just completing the initial orbital scan when our aft power coils suddenly exploded. We attempted to compensate with the ventral relays, but there wasn't enough time. The ship got caught in the sphere's gravity well . . . and down we went. We dropped like a bloody stone."

Geordi whistled softly. "It's a miracle the ship's superstructure survived a crash like that."

Scott's face clouded over. "It nearly didn't. Franklin and I were the only ones to survive the crash."

Geordi grunted, trying to imagine the man's feelings when he realized he was still alive—but that so many others had perished.

Swallowing, he asked another question. "What made you think of using the transporter's pattern buffer to stay alive?"

Scott shook his head. "Ye know what they say about necessity being the mother of invention. We didnae have enough supplies to wait for a rescue . . . so I had to think of something."

"But locking it into a diagnostic cycle to keep the signal from degrading . . . and cross-connecting the phase inducers to provide a regenerative power source . . ." Geordi couldn't have concealed his admiration if he'd wanted to. "It's brilliant."

Scott sighed. "I'm afraid it was only fifty percent brilliant, lad. Ensign Franklin deserved better."

Noting the man's sadness, Geordi changed the subject—to something Scott could get excited about. "I think you're going to like the twenty-fourth century, Captain Scott. We've made some pretty amazing advances in the last eighty years."

It worked. Scott seemed to perk up a bit as they entered the turbolift. Looking around the compartment, he nodded approvingly.

"Aye. From what I can see, ye've got a fine ship here, Mr. La Forge. A real beauty. In fact, I must admit to being a mite overwhelmed."

Geordi chuckled. "Wait until you see the holodeck!"

As the doors closed, Scott gave him a look of mingled surprise and curiosity. "The holodeck?" he wondered.

Chapter Four

"So WHAT DO YE THINK, LASS?" asked Scott.

Beverly Crusher, chief medical officer of the Starship *Enterprise,* looked down at her latest patient and shook her head.

"You're a treasure, Captain Scott. A real find. The only person ever to spend seventy-five years cycling around in a transporter and live to tell of it. Now hold still, will you?"

Sitting on a biobed in sickbay, Scott winced as the doctor examined his injured limb. "Easy for you to say," he told her. "Your arm hasn't been broken for the last seventy-five years. *Ouch.*"

Chuckling at his quip, Crusher picked up her medical tricorder and ran it over Scott's arm—just as Geordi entered sickbay. She raised her head just long enough to smile at him and go back to her business.

"Hi, Doc," said the chief engineer. "Hi, Captain Scott. See? I told you I'd be right back."

"So ye did," agreed Scott.

The doctor consulted her readouts. "You've got a hairline fracture of the humerus," she said. Shutting off the device, she added: "It'll ache for a few days, but after that it should be fine."

"Thank you," said Scott, smiling appreciatively. In his day, Crusher decided, he must have been something of a ladies' man. Even now, he had a disarming twinkle in his eye—one that might turn a woman's head if she wasn't careful.

As if to confirm her suspicions, Scott turned to Geordi and declared: "Well, I'll say this for your *Enterprise*. The doctors are a fair sight *prettier* than what I was used to."

The remark was a little too obvious for Crusher's taste. Still and all, she couldn't help but smile. "Flattery will get you nowhere," she lied, depositing the tricorder into one of the pockets in her lab coat.

"I apologize if I was out of line," said Scott— suddenly a good deal more earnest. "But I cannae help it. A beautiful woman will loosen my tongue faster than a whole case of Saurian brandy."

That was no line, the doctor realized. That was a confession.

Before she could reply, however, the sickbay doors opened to admit another visitor. This time, it was the man in charge of the *Enterprise*.

"Captain Scott," said Geordi, as dutiful as ever, "this is Captain Picard."

Picard crossed the room and extended his hand to

the newcomer, smiling broadly. "Jean-Luc Picard, Captain Scott. Welcome aboard."

Scott clasped the captain's hand as warmly as it was offered. "Thank ye, sir. Of all the ships that could have found me, I'm glad it was yers. But—if ye dinnae mind—call me Scotty."

Picard nodded. "Very well. How are you feeling . . . Scotty?"

Scott looked to Beverly. "I dinnae know. How am I feeling, Doctor?"

Crusher grunted in mock-seriousness. "Well," she said, "other than a couple of bumps and bruises and a slightly battered arm, I'd say you feel fine for a man of a hundred and forty-seven."

Scott cast Picard a rakish look. "How about that? An' I dinnae feel a *day* over a hundred and twenty!"

Picard grinned at Scott politely. However, he didn't join in the bantering. As Crusher knew from long experience, that just wasn't the captain's style.

"I must say," Picard commented, "I was more than a little surprised when Commander Riker informed me that you were aboard the *Jenolen*. Our records didn't list you as one of their crew."

Scott's smile faded a little. "I wasn't actually a member of the crew, sir. Truth to tell, I was just a . . . a passenger." He winced again, just as he had when Crusher had touched a sore spot on his arm. "I was heading for Norpin Five, y'see, to settle down and enjoy my . . . *retirement.*"

He spat out the last word as if it left a bad taste in his mouth. And maybe it did, Crusher mused. Obviously, the man found the whole idea of retirement an embarassment.

"I see," remarked the captain. "Well, I would very much enjoy the opportunity to discuss your career at some point. History is one of my hobbies . . . and I'm sure you have some fascinating insights into the events of your time."

"I dinnae know if I'd call them fascinating exactly," Scott replied, smiling at each of them in turn. "But I'd be happy to answer your questions."

"Good," said Picard. "I look forward to it. Unfortunately, I must return to the bridge now."

"I know the feeling," Scott said. "Duty calls. I've been called to the bridge a few times myself, y'know."

He's asserting himself, thought Crusher. Reminding us that he was once important too.

"So I understand," the captain assured him. Turning to Geordi, he said in a somewhat less casual tone: "Commander, we need to begin a full analysis of the Dyson Sphere."

Geordi nodded. "I'll get right on it, sir."

Finally, Picard refocused his attention on Crusher's patient. "Again, welcome aboard, Mr. Scott." And with that, he took his leave of them.

A moment later, Geordi turned to Scott. "You heard the captain. I have to get back to engineering to start that analysis."

Scott's face lit up at the word. "*Engineering,* lad? I thought ye'd never ask!"

And before Crusher could stop him, he'd moved down off the biobed to accompany Geordi. However, the doctor wasn't about to give Scott the run of the ship—not after what he'd been through. Though he was in generally good health, there was no telling what kind of long-term effects that kind of experience would have on a human body.

"Just a minute," she said, placing a restraining hand on the older man's shoulder. "Where do you think you're going?"

Scott looked at her, puzzled. "What is it, lass? Ye've finished yer tests, have ye nae?"

"True," Crusher conceded. "But you've had quite a shock to your system and I don't want you to push yourself too hard. The first thing you're going to do is get some rest."

Scott seemed on the verge of protesting—until Geordi intervened. "We're pretty busy right now anyway, Captain Scott. But I'd be happy to give you a tour of engineering a little later, when the doctor says it's okay."

Scott looked from one of them to the other. Faced with uniform resistance, he sighed. "Aye," he said in a resigned tone, even managing a little smile. "When the doctor says it's okay."

"Great," said Geordi. "See you then."

As they watched him exit through the sickbay doors, Beverly turned to Scott. "I'll ask for an ensign to show you to your quarters," she said.

"Whatever ye say," he told her. He was clearly disappointed.

But Crusher wasn't about to give in. If all went well, there would be plenty of time for Scott to see engineering and whatever else he liked—later.

By now, Ensign Kane had expected Commander Riker to be treating him a little better. But he wasn't.

Far from it. Kane was still mired in cargo duty—much to the detriment of his status among the other ensigns.

Kane hated to admit he was wrong. He hated being shown up. So instead of keeping his mouth shut, since that was what had gotten him into this hole in the first place, he opted to dig a little deeper.

"I'm telling you," he said, commanding the attention of the other half-dozen male ensigns in the rec room, "the man's going to come crawling to me on his knees, begging my forgiveness. Just wait and see."

Tranh, who'd graduated just behind Kane at the Academy, shook his head and chuckled. "Sure he will. And then we'll all put on dresses and do a little jig."

That got the rest of them laughing—even Sousa, who'd turned out to be Kane's best friend in this sorry bunch. Kane could feel his cheeks growing hotter with each passing moment.

"Go ahead," he said, putting on the best show of confidence that he could muster. "Laugh all you want. You're going to look pretty funny dancing around in those dresses."

That got the chuckles going his way. He smiled, building on his progress. One thing Darrin Kane knew how to do was work a crowd.

"Tell you what, though," he said. "When I'm up there on the bridge, impressing the hell out of the captain, I won't forget my friends. I'll make sure you get *twice* the recommended—"

Before he could finish, a voice rang out in the rec. "Ensign Kane . . . this is Commander Riker."

As far as the ensigns were concerned, it might as well have been the voice of God. Riker was the man on whom all their careers depended, the single most important factor in whether they realized their dreams or spent the rest of their lives as second bananas.

Kane just smiled. Finally, he thought. He's had his conversation with Picard and he's calling to make his atonement.

Well, Kane wasn't going to make it easy for him. Instead of answering right away, he took the time to grin at each of the others in turn, as if to say: *You see? I told you he'd come around.*

"Ensign Kane?" Riker called again.

Clearing his throat, the ensign responded in a casual tone. "Aye, sir?"

A pause. "Ensign . . . am I catching you at a bad time?"

Kane's grin widened. "No, sir."

"Because if I am," Riker continued, "I can always find someone else to give this assignment to."

The ensign straightened at the word *assignment*. This was what he'd been waiting for. He didn't want to blow it.

But by the same token, he didn't want to lose the entertainment value of this little scene. It was almost as important to him that he regain his preeminence among his peers as that he get his career on firmer footing.

"No, sir," Kane assured the first officer. "I'm ready, willing and able." But he put an ironic spin on the words, eliciting muffled sniggers and head shaking from his companions.

"Good," said Riker. "In that case, you're on duty as of right now. I want you to report to sickbay."

Kane felt as if he'd just hit some turbulence. "Sickbay, sir?" What in blazes was happening there that was so important they needed *him* to take care of it? Weren't there nurses for that sort of thing?

"That's right," Riker confirmed. "Sickbay. There's a Captain Scott there. I want you to escort him to his room."

Suddenly, the snickering stopped. Kane looked around at his fellow ensigns. They were actually too astonished to laugh.

Next to this, cargo duty was an honor. Escorting someone to his room . . . was there a less vital job? He couldn't think of one.

"Ensign?" Riker barked. "Do I need to repeat myself?

Kane ground his teeth together. This wasn't the way it was supposed to work. He was supposed to be on top here.

"No, sir," he muttered finally. "Sickbay. Captain Scott."

"Immediately," the first officer told him. "Captain Scott will be waiting."

Then silence—ridiculing him, crushing him beneath its boot. Kane wanted to fill it with curses, but that would just have made matters worse. It would only have underlined his humiliation.

Tranh smiled—too embarrassed for Kane to really rub it in. Instead, he said softly: "I guess we can keep the dresses in mothballs . . . eh, Ensign?"

He could have tolerated Tranh's scorn. But his sympathy . . . his pity . . . it was almost more than Kane could bear.

He wanted to hit Tranh. He wanted to make him

hurt as bad as he was hurting. But he restrained himself. An assault on another ensign wouldn't look very good on his record, and there was still a possibility that his record would be important to him one day.

"Hey," said Sousa, putting a reassuring hand on his arm. "It's no big deal, Kane. It's all right."

But it wasn't all right—not by a long shot. Shrugging off Sousa's hand, he got up and crossed the room, heading for the exit. He was seething; it was all he could do not to boil over.

He'd thought things were bad before. But now the situation was rapidly becoming . . . intolerable.

Scott smiled. The ensign assigned to show him his quarters was about as polite as they came. It was good to know that Starfleet was still choosy about who it permitted to serve on its flagships.

Of course, it was possible that Ensign Kane was an anomaly among his peers, but Scott hoped not. He would have hated it if the human race had gone downhill from the level achieved in the twenty-third century.

"Here we are, sir," said Kane. He stopped in front of a sliding door, which didn't look a whole lot different than the sliding doors on Scott's *Enterprise*. "After you, sir."

Polite all right, Scott observed. He nodded approvingly, but the lad was too disciplined even to smile. All he did was wait patiently for the older man to enter ahead of him.

The doors whooshed open automatically, of course. A moment later, Scott saw the quarters that had been set aside for him . . . and gasped.

Before he knew it, Kane had launched into the grand tour. "You'll find the closet back there, with a full wardrobe in your size. And this," he said, gesturing, "is the food replicator . . . and your computer terminal . . ."

Scott looked around the room in astonishment. "Good lord, man. Where have ye put me?"

Kane turned to stare at him blankly. "These are standard guest quarters, sir." A pause. "I can try to find something bigger if you wish."

Scott's eyes widened. "Bigger? Ye misunderstand me, lad. Why, in my day, even an admiral would nae have had such quarters on a starship. In fact," he went on, his mind seeking familiar things, "I remember a time when we had to transport the Dohlman of Elaas to Troyius." He chuckled. "You never heard such whining and complaining from a grown woman in all your life."

"Uh . . . right," responded Kane, as courteous as ever. "The holodecks, Ten-Forward and the gymnasium are all at your disposal." He indicated the desktop terminal. "The computer can tell you how to find them. Until we issue you a combadge, just use this"—another gesture—"communications panel if you need anything."

But Scott wasn't paying very close attention. Again, he was dredging up memories. "You know," he said, "these quarters remind me of a hotel room I once had on Argelius. Oh, now, there was a planet . . . everything a man could want, right at his fingertips. 'Course on our first visit, I ran into a wee bit o'trouble there, but . . ."

"Uh, excuse me, sir," said Kane.

Scott stopped. "Aye, lad?"

"I have to return to duty, sir." The ensign was still smiling politely . . . but now he seemed too polite. As if he was just putting on a facade, and had been all along.

Scott frowned. What a fool he'd been. Ensign Kane wasn't interested in the Dohlman of Elaas or the accommodations on Argelius or any other stories he had to tell. Scott could see that now. All Kane wanted to do was discharge his burden and get on with his business.

"Sorry to trouble ye," said the older man.

The ensign didn't miss a beat. "No trouble at all, sir. Will there be anything else?"

Scott shook his head, his exuberance punctured. "No, nothing. Thank you, Mr. Kane."

The man didn't linger any longer than he had to. A moment later, the doors slid closed behind him and Scott was alone.

Alone. In this gigantic suite. Aboard a vast and unfamiliar ship.

He sighed and sat down on the overstuffed couch they'd given him. He looked around. Then he sighed again. On the *Enterprise*—the one he'd cut his teeth on—the hum of the engines had been audible everywhere on the ship, no matter where you were. After a while, he'd had trouble sleeping anywhere else, because he missed that soothing hum.

He didn't think he'd sleep well *here*. The place was as quiet as a tomb. Maybe there were engines humming somewhere on this ship, but you couldn't prove it by his cabin. Nor, he suspected, anywhere else outside of engineering.

Scott suddenly felt very lost—like a child who'd strayed from his parents' side. And he knew why, too. There was nothing for him to do here.

All his life, he had prided himself on his usefulness. If you wanted something done, you gave it to Scotty. People had called him a genius, a mechanical wizard, a bloody miracle worker.

The point was, he could make things happen. That is, if he was given a chance. And here . . . here and *now* . . . there was no chance.

This *Enterprise* had an engineer already. And even if it didn't, he wouldn't be nearly equal to the task—not with his incomplete and antiquated understanding of modern technology. Damn . . . he'd mistaken an EPS power tap for a data conduit. He could've gotten himself *killed* making a mistake like that.

Maybe if he'd had a family . . . if he'd settled down . . . he would've found some other way to define himself. But the only children he could ever rightly call his own were the engines of Jim Kirk's *Enterprise*—and those were long gone, like everything else he'd known and loved.

What to do Montgomery, what to do? Scott thought. Lord knew he had to do *something* or he'd go berserk. And he couldn't believe that he alone had been preserved—out of all those poor souls on the *Jenolen* —just so he could slowly and painfully lose his marbles.

He perked up at the thought. He *had* been preserved, hadn't he? And if that was the case, there had to be a purpose to it. Maybe it wasn't apparent just yet, but a purpose nonetheless.

"Aye," he said out loud. "Old Montgomery Scott is

nae done yet. Somewhere out there in that great expanse of stars, maybe even somewhere on this ship, there's a piece o' machinery that needs my gentle touch. And if I'm patient, I'll find it."

Brave words, he thought. And even if he wasn't quite sure he believed them, they sure sounded good.

Chapter Five

PICARD USED the back of his bare left hand to wipe away a rivulet of sweat that was threatening to run into his eyes. Then, with ease born of practice, he replaced his mask over his face and saluted his opponent with his blade.

A few meters away, Riker returned the salute and dropped into his crouch. Perhaps a bit too low, the captain judged. But then, his first officer was a comparative novice at the fine art of fencing.

"En garde," Picard announced, taking a step forward.

Riker held his ground, not even moving his point. That took discipline, the captain knew. A rare quality in beginners.

Not that he had any intention of rewarding it. Taking another step, Picard lunged—not so much a serious attack as a means of getting his opponent to move backward, and thereby make him more vulnerable.

But Riker must have seen through his strategy, because he didn't cooperate. Instead of retreating, he flipped the captain's blade to the side—not much really, just enough to make it miss him—and launched a counterassault of his own.

It started out looking like a simple lunge, but it very quickly extended itself into a running attack. And it caught the more experienced man flatfooted. It was all Picard could do to swat at Riker's point, keeping it from finding its target, as he back-pedaled the length of the fencing strip.

As the captain retreated beyond the end line, his adversary made one last, desperate thrust—and came up just short. Another inch and he'd have scored a touch. And a brilliant touch at that, Picard mused.

"Bravo," he shouted, as both of them slowed down —the captain going backward, his first officer going forward. "I see you've been practicing behind my back."

Riker smiled through the mesh of his mask. "You make it sound dishonest," he laughed.

"It *is,*" Picard rejoined. "But all's fair in love and fencing, I suppose."

As they took up their positions again, the captain found himself at a disadvantage. According to the rules, he had to begin again near the end line. If he retreated past it again, a touch would be counted against him automatically. But he'd be damned before he'd let that happen.

"En garde?" suggested Riker.

Picard nodded. "Indeed."

No sooner had the word left his mouth than he feinted—an attempt to move his opponent backward and give himself some breathing room. But as before, Riker wasn't buying it. He just stood there, refusing to budge an inch.

"There's no shame in retreat, Will," said the captain.

Riker chuckled. "None in being aggressive, either."

Without warning, the bigger man lunged. But this time, Picard was ready for him. Sweeping Riker's blade aside with a flourish, the captain brought his own back on line—just in time to plant his point in his first officer's unguarded chest.

"Alas!" barked Picard, for a brief second once more an arrogant young Frenchman in his master's fencing den.

Riker sighed as he took off his mask. His hair was plastered over his forehead. "Nice touch, sir."

Removing his own mask as well, Picard inclined his head slightly by way of acknowledgment. "Thank you, Will. But next time, it might pay for you to back off a little . . . give me a false sense of security . . . and *then* come at me."

His first officer nodded. "I'll remember that."

The captain tilted his head to indicate the replicator in the corner of the gymnasium. "Care to take a break?"

Riker looked as if he'd have liked to continue. But he said: "Sure. Why not?" And tucking his mask beneath his sword arm, he followed his superior to the replicator.

"Tea," said Picard, as he approached the device.

"Earl Grey. Hot." He turned to his second-in-command. "And you, Will?"

"Mountain stream water. As cold as it'll get without freezing."

A moment later, the replicator complied with their requests. The captain removed the drinks, handed the frigid one to Riker and took a sip of his tea.

"So," he began, starting off with a feint, "how is Captain Scott faring? I trust you left him in good hands?"

"The best," said the first officer. "I've asked Geordi to take him under his wing."

"Good," Picard commented. "After all he's been through, he deserves whatever help we can give him."

Riker had fallen for the feint. Now it was time to move in—to pursue his ulterior motive in asking the younger man down here.

"Will, I had a visit in my ready room not so long ago. From Ensign Kane."

He saw Riker stiffen slightly at the mention of the man's name. "So that's why you've been avoiding me," he said. "And what did Kane have to say?"

"I think you know," said Picard, though he went on to supply the details anyway. "That you're being unfair with him. That you're denying him a chance to sharpen his skills. That you, for some reason, *resent* him."

The first officer met his gaze. "I *do* resent him," he conceded. "I resent him a *lot.*" A pause. "But that's not why I'm treating him differently from the others. Ensign Kane has a lot to learn when it comes to respecting his superior officers."

The captain tried to read into Riker's statement. "Ambition is hardly a crime, Will. Otherwise, we'd both be guilty of it ourselves. And for that matter, so would every officer in the fleet."

"I'm not just talking about ambition, sir. I'm talking about arrogance. A lack of esteem for authority—for tradition."

Picard frowned. "A severe enough lack to put him at the bottom of the duty roster?"

"That's right," said his Number One. But he wasn't forthcoming with any details. And the captain *wanted* details.

"As you know," he told Riker, "I graduated from the Academy with Darrin Kane's father. I've known the ensign since he was a boy—"

"Perhaps not as well as you think, sir." The first officer's cheeks had darkened by a shade. He took a second or two to compose himself before speaking again. "Captain . . . when I agreed to become first officer of this ship, it was with the understanding that I believed passionately in certain things. Now, you can scrutinize the way I'm handling Ensign Kane or you can trust me to do my job. But if it's the former . . ."

Riker didn't finish the sentence. He didn't have to.

Picard eyed him. "You feel that strongly about it, do you?"

"I do, sir." He stood his ground—just as he had on the fencing strip.

It was up to the captain to allow him that position or to try to move him—at the risk of losing him. Ultimately, it came down to this: *Should* he move him? Was it or was it not his job to intervene?

Picard made his decision. "You do what you think is best," he told his first officer. "As far as I'm concerned, the matter is closed."

Riker looked appreciative. "Thank you, sir."

"Ensign Kane . . ."

At first, Kane thought he was merely caught in the throes of a nightmare. Riker's voice seemed to boom across a dark and foreboding landscape, starting landslides and making tall crags quake. And no matter where he ran or how he tried to hide, he couldn't escape it.

"Ensign Kane . . ."

It was like thunder, cascading down from a steel-gray nest of roiling storm clouds . . . huge, deafening, crushing him beneath its weight . . .

"Ensign Kane!"

Kane shot upright. He looked around, his throat dry and hot with fear.

He was in his cabin, he realized. His cabin on the *Enterprise*, not the nightmare world of his imaginings. And that voice . . . it was Riker, all right. The *real* Riker. But why would . . .?

And then he caught sight of the chronometer on his desk, and he had his answer. He was ten minutes late for his shift—and still in bed. Tearing aside his blanket, he swung his bare feet out onto the floor.

Damn, damn, *damn* . . .

"Aye, sir. This is Kane. I've overslept, sir."

"Really?" said Riker's intercom voice. "I'd never have guessed."

Darting across the room to his chest of drawers, the

ensign pulled out a fresh uniform. His heart was pounding a staccato beat on his rib cage.

"I'm sorry, Commander," he spat out. "I don't know how it happened. I thought I asked the computer for a wake-up call . . ."

"You didn't," Riker pointed out. "I checked."

Kane cursed as he pulled on his red-and-black garb. That did it. Bad enough Riker hated him; now he'd given him an excuse. The more black marks the first officer could put on his record, the easier it would be to keep him down.

Of course, it wouldn't have occurred in the first place if he'd gotten to bed at a reasonable time. But he'd been so furious at his assignment to babysit the old man that he'd stayed up in Ten-Forward until the wee hours . . . tossing down the synthehol and thinking of ways to get even.

"It won't happen again, sir, I assure you. I'll be down to the cargo hold in just a couple of minutes." The ensign *hated* the idea of having to kowtow to Riker . . . of having to make nice. He *detested* it. But the man held Kane's fate in his hands; there was no way around it.

"Don't bother," the first officer told him.

Kane had been pulling on one of his pants legs; he stopped in mid-tug. "I beg your pardon, sir?"

"I said don't bother. You won't be going to the cargo hold today."

A smile spread over the ensign's face. Don't tell me he's *finally* had his talk with Picard, he mused. Don't tell me I'm finally going to get what's coming to me . . . !

"Where will I be going, then . . . sir?" He pulled his pants leg up the rest of the way, but he was no longer in quite so much of a hurry.

He could almost hear Riker saying: *the bridge.* In fact, he was so sure he'd be hearing those two wonderful, long-overdue words that he almost missed the words Riker did utter.

"Main shuttlebay. Deck Four."

"What . . . ?" The ensign didn't mean to blurt it out. But he did, and loud enough for it to be heard over the intercom system.

"Main shuttlebay," Riker repeated. "Something wrong with your hearing, Ensign?"

"No . . . nothing, sir."

"Believe me," Riker added, "I wouldn't take you off your regular duty unless there was a good reason. But Coburn just had an attack of appendicitis and someone needs to replace him." A pause. "Don't worry. It'll just be for a while. When Coburn's well again, you can resume your normal schedule."

In the silence that followed, Kane just stood there. Then he pounded his fist on the top of his dresser—so hard that the synthetic material shivered. The nightmare wasn't over, he thought. It was just beginning.

Scott knew he was supposed to rest, but he couldn't have stayed in his suite much longer without losing his mind. He felt the need to get out . . . to see a bit more of this gargantuan ship and what she had to offer. And while the holodeck sounded interesting, that wasn't the kind of thing he needed. Not right now, anyway.

The same for Ten-Forward—whatever that was—

and the gymnasium. He hadn't exercised for seventy-five years; it wouldn't kill him to put it off a little longer.

What he really wanted to see were some machines. Machines that harnessed energy and machines that used it . . . machines that made things go and made things stop . . . machines without which this wonder of a starship couldn't have hoped to function. That's what he yearned for. That's what made his pulse rush, and always had.

On the other hand, he knew he wasn't authorized to see such things. He was supposed to be resting, not fiddling. Apparently, they didn't know him very well. Telling Montgomery Scott not to do something was tantamount to an open invitation.

On the other hand, he wanted to remain close to home—close to his quarters on Deck Seven. That way, if he was apprehended somewhere he shouldn't be, he could always claim he'd just gotten a little lost.

Of course, his first choice of a destination would have been the engine room. But there would be too many people there now, what with everyone engaged in analyzing the Dyson Sphere. Better to choose a less populated place, where he could lose himself for a while.

A place like Shuttlebay One. If he couldn't get his hands on the engines that drove the *Enterprise*—not yet, anyway—poring over a shuttle would be the next best thing.

As he left his quarters, Scott walked down the corridor as if there were no reason for him not to. People glanced at his sling, but if they recognized him by it, they didn't let on. When he reached the turbolift station, the doors opened for him and he got on.

So far so good, he told himself. "Shuttlebay One," he told the computer, just the way he'd seen Commander La Forge do it on their way down to sickbay.

He'd barely completed the command, it seemed, before the doors opened again at his destination. He nodded his head in admiration. The lifts on his *Enterprise* had never been that quick or that smooth.

Emerging into the corridor, he looked both ways . . . and found Shuttlebay One just a few meters to his left. Again, he made his way in that direction as if he were just another cog in the great, twenty-fourth-century machine. And again, no one stopped him to say otherwise.

The shuttlebay entrance was just as accommodating. It yawned wide at his approach, unveiling a veritable feast for his engineer's eyes: a space as big as an entire deck on the *Jenolen*, stocked with nearly two dozen shuttlecraft—some large and some small, gleaming in the overhead illumination like a herd of heavenly beasts.

"Damn," he said. He couldn't help but grin at the sight of them.

Crossing the large, open space in the center of the facility, he put his hand out and caressed the metal skin of the nearest vehicle. It was unexpectedly warm to the touch.

What's more, it was a lot more streamlined than the shuttles of Scott's day, with their sharp corners and boxy designs. The machine before him was so sleek, its lines so clean and pleasing to the eye, that it seemed almost unnatural for it to be standing still. It should have been gliding through space, plummeting through the upper atmosphere of some planet the way a rare pearl falls through still water.

Scott read the name on its flank, rendered in a graceful, flowing hand. The name was *Christopher*. He grunted happily. That would be Sean Jeffrey Christopher, the man who headed the first successful Earth-Titan probe in the early part of the twenty-first century—and the son of Captain John Christopher, who was very briefly an unintended and temporally inconvenient guest of the *Enterprise.*

But had it not been for Scott, who found a way to return Christopher to his timeline minutes before he encountered the *Enterprise,* there would have been no Sean Jeffrey Christopher—and quite possibly, no United Federation of Planets. For if the expedition to Saturn's satellite had failed, Earth's space program may have never have developed into the organization known as Starfleet. And if Starfleet didn't exist, how could there ever have been a Federation?

Hearing the shuffle of feet on the deck behind him, Scott turned—and saw a familiar face. It was the ensign who'd shown him to his quarters the day before. The one who'd been so polite.

What was his name? Crane? No, something else . . .

He snapped his fingers. "Kane."

The ensign nodded, looking at him warily. "That's right, sir." He paused. "Uh, are you authorized to be here?"

Scott winked at him. "To tell the truth, laddie, I'm not authorized to scratch my nose on this ship. But the way I look at it, ye cannae sit in yer room and count the rivets in the bulkheads when there's a whole new world right outside yer door. If ye catch my meaning."

The ensign frowned. "Kane to security," he said, never taking his eyes off the older man. "I've got an intruder in the main shuttlebay by the name of Captain Scott. I think he needs an escort back to his quarters."

Scott felt as if he'd been stabbed in the back. "Now that," he told the ensign, "was nae necessary. Nae necessary at all."

Kane shrugged. "I've got enough problems of my own without going out on a limb for an unauthorized visitor." His mouth quirked into something like a grin, if a bitter one. "If you catch my meaning."

Before Scott could respond to the ensign's impertinence, Lieutenant Worf had arrived with a couple of his security officers. The older man braced himself for some typical Klingon heavy-handedness.

But it never materialized. Worf's manner was almost gentle as he said: "Will you come with me, sir?"

Scott harrumphed. "Well," he replied, casting a withering look back at Ensign Kane, "when ye ask so nicely, lad, it's difficult to refuse."

And surrounded by security officers, he made his way back to his big, empty suite. But he was already planning his next escapade. Now that he'd gotten a taste of what was out there, he wasn't about to sit and stare at four walls, no matter what Dr. Crusher said.

For a couple of hours, he decided, he'd lie low. Then, when no one expected it, he'd take another little trip. And this time, it would be to the place he *really* wanted to visit.

Chapter Six

DOWN IN ENGINEERING, a handful of engineers were working at consoles and checking displays, each man and woman intent on carrying out the series of tests assigned to him or her. Geordi was all but oblivious to the activity, however. He'd been given a task of his own, for which he was laying the groundwork on his desktop monitor.

"Commander La Forge?"

He looked up and saw Kerry Bartel standing at the entrance to his office. "Come on in," said Geordi. "Just don't get too comfortable. I've got a job for you."

"And that is?" asked Bartel, a tall, blond woman— and a real go-getter, in Geordi's estimate.

The chief engineer swiveled his monitor around so Bartel could get a look at the graphic on it. "The bridge wants a complete spectrographic scan of the sphere and we'll need all the sensors to be synchronized. Unfortunately, I can't recalibrate the aft array with the warp engines in operation."

The woman nodded. "I get it. You want me to shut them down."

"That's exactly what I want you to do."

Bartel smiled. "Aye, sir. Consider it done."

As he headed for the engine core, Geordi went back to work on his terminal. Truth to tell, he was eager to perform this spectrographic analysis. He was as curious about the sphere as anyone else.

The chief engineer was so intent on setting up the scan that he barely heard the sudden outbreak of conversation outside. It registered only on the periphery of his consciousness—an unusual occurrence when there was so much to do, but nothing that really required any action from him.

His people were highly trained professionals. The conversation would end in a moment or two, and the men or women involved would get back to work.

At least, that was the way it was *supposed* to happen. Unfortunately, it didn't. Not only did the conversation not stop, it seemed to be getting closer to his office—and involving more and more people as it approached.

A little exasperated, Geordi listened more closely. This had better be something interesting, he thought, or heads will roll.

"Can I help you, sir?" asked one of the voices. He recognized it as Bartel's.

"I dinnae think so, lass. But I'll let you know if you can do something for me *later*—I promise ye that."

Geordi scowled. He recognized *that* voice too.

Getting up, he moved to the threshold of his office and peered around the corner.

His suspicions were confirmed. Captain Scott had cut a swathe through engineering and was now making his way toward the warp core—accompanied by a very concerned Kerry Bartel.

As Geordi approached them to intervene, the older man was regarding the pulsating core with genuine pleasure and affection. A distinctly *paternal* pleasure and affection.

"Sir," Bartel argued, trying to interpose herself between Scott and the core, "this area is off-limits, restricted to—"

"It's all right," said Geordi, cutting the young engineer short. "I'll handle it, Bartel."

The engineer frowned. "If you say so, Commander."

Geordi nodded. "I say so."

Acquiescing, Bartel left. Geordi considered his unexpected visitor, who was slowly walking around the warp core, taking everything in. He sighed.

Be diplomatic, he told himself. Be gentle. He means well. And remember, he's been through a tough experience.

"Captain Scott," he ventured, "this . . . uh, really isn't a good time—"

The older man turned to him and smiled affably. He was now wearing an *Enterprise* combadge. "We're in engineering, lad. And in engineering, ye've got to call me Scotty."

"Okay. Scotty then. This really isn't a good time for a tour. We're in the middle of—"

Scott seemed oblivious to what he was saying—or

trying to say. "Are ye still using cobalt lathanide for the constrictor coils?" he asked.

"Uh, right." Geordi thrust his chin out. "Sir. *Scotty*. We're running a phase seven survey of the Dyson Sphere. I *really* can't take the time for a tour right now."

Scott turned and looked at him as if he'd just offered him a cup of antimatter. "I'm not here for a tour, lad," he explained. "I'm here to *help.*"

Geordi was surprised. It showed, he was afraid.

"That's, er . . . very kind of you. But I think we can handle it."

Scott moved quickly to the pool table–like situations monitor. Geordi followed, wondering what the man was up to now.

"I figured," said the older man, "that since I'm the only one here who's had any experience at all with the Dyson Sphere, I could be of some assistance. You know, in getting yer investigation off on the right foot."

Geordi hesitated. "Well . . ." For a moment, he considered that Scott might be right. He *was* the only person alive who'd done any real research on the sphere.

Scott looked at him askance. "I was a Starfleet engineer for fifty-two years, Mr. La Forge. I think I'm still of some use—am I nae?"

"You're right, Captain Scott. We'd appreciate any help you can give us."

Scott beamed. Was that a twinkle of surprise in his eye—surprise that he had actually been allowed to remain here? Geordi couldn't be sure.

"Good," said Scott, rubbing his hands together

eagerly. "Let's get to work then, shall we?" And he turned to the situations monitor to do just that.

As Geordi joined him, he had a feeling he was going to regret this.

Captain's Log, Stardate 46125.3
At my request, Starfleet Command has dispatched three science vessels to make a lengthy study of the Dyson Sphere. Until they arrive, however, the *Enterprise* will continue to gather preliminary data on this remarkable construct.

Standing at the aft science station where he'd spent the last several hours, Data pointed to his monitor, which displayed a cross section of the Dyson Sphere. The section revealed a captive star and a thin atmosphere adhering to the inside of the sphere. Computer information on the object's vital statistics was visible in list form off to the side.

"You see, sir?" asked the android. "Sensor readings indicate the presence of a G-type star at the center of the Dyson Sphere. There also appears to be a class-M atmosphere clinging to the interior surface."

Picard, who had been hovering about his second officer periodically, nodded his head. "Then there *is* a possibility," he concluded, his voice charged with excitement.

"It would appear that way," Data responded.

The captain's eyes narrowed as he stared at the statistics on the monitor. "Is there any *indication* that the sphere is inhabited? Any positive evidence that life still exists in there?"

"Not as yet, sir," the android told him. "Our preliminary data indicates that the sphere is still *capable* of supporting life, but we have been unable to find definite signs of current habitation."

Picard grunted thoughtfully. Data had seldom seen him so intrigued by a scientific discovery. He said so.

"Intrigued?" the human echoed. "I'll say I'm intrigued. That's why I went out into space in the first place, Data. That's why I spent twenty years and more on the *Stargazer,* and why I agreed to serve as captain of the *Enterprise.* For the possibility of glimpsing a form of life so different that I could not otherwise have imagined it."

Picard turned to the main viewscreen, where the sphere was displayed in all its gargantuan glory. The android followed his gaze.

"Whoever built that might qualify as such a life-form, Data. And if there is an opportunity to speak with him, her or it . . . to understand what drove them to encapsulate a star for their own use . . ." He shrugged. "I will do everything in my power to seize that opportunity. To gain that understanding." He turned back to the android and smiled. "That is, after all, my job."

The android didn't quite know what to say to that. His own thirst for knowledge was part of his programming. Yet, he didn't think he could have expressed the desire in words as well as the captain had.

Picard focused on the station monitor anew. The muscles in his temples rippled with concentration. Finally, a conclusion was reached, a plan of action devised.

"Send out a series of class-four probes to survey the far side of the sphere, Mr. Data. Perhaps we'll have more luck with them."

"Aye, sir," said the android. And before another second could go by, he had initiated the launch of the first probe.

Leaning forward over the situations monitor, with Captain Scott doing the same thing right beside him, Geordi wondered if a spectrographic analysis had ever taken so long in the history of Starfleet. Or maybe it wasn't really taking as long as he thought. Maybe it only seemed that way.

Not that he had any problem with Scott's attitude. The man couldn't be more cheerful or more excited. But in his efforts to be helpful, he was really getting on everyone's nerves.

Trying to focus on the monitor and not his frustration, Geordi said: "Okay. The lateral sensors are on-line. Mr. Krause, adjust the frequency stabilization on the main deflector dish. It's out of synch with the aft sensors."

"Aye, sir," said Krause, doing as he was told. As Geordi watched, he brought the frequency stabilization and the sensors back into synch.

"Okay," said the chief engineer. Now—"

"Laddie," Scott interrupted.

Reluctantly, Geordi turned to him. He had a serious glint in his eye.

"Yes, Captain Scott . . . er, Scotty?"

"Ye need to phase-lock the warp fields within three percent or they'll become unstable," said Scott.

Geordi shook his head as if to clear it. "What?"

Working the console, Scotty showed him what he meant. "Here, I'll show ye. Y'see, the warp field is—"

But no sooner had Scott touched the controls than the monitor table suddenly sounded an alarm. The man looked around helplessly.

Moving quickly, Geordi corrected the situation. It didn't take much, but it was yet another delay. And he didn't have all the time in the universe to get this done.

"I dinnae understand . . ." Scott began.

Geordi explained, trying to hang onto what was left of his forbearance. "We use a five-phase autocontainment field now. It's meant to operate *above* three percent."

Scott seemed rattled—but only for a moment. Then he was his confident self again. "Ah," he replied. "Well. That would make all the difference in the world now, would it nae?"

"Commander La Forge?"

Geordi turned in response to Bartel's call. She and two other engineers were working on the darkened warp core.

"Yes?" La Forge responded.

"We're nearly done with the recalibration, Commander. We can restart the engines in ten minutes."

"Thanks," said Geordi. "Glad to hear it." He watched as Bartel and the others returned to their labors.

"Ye know," Scott interjected, "speaking o' restarting the engines . . . I remember a time when the old *Enterprise* was spiralling in toward Psi Two Thousand. The captain—Captain Kirk, that is—wanted to try a cold start of the warp engines. But I told him it was nae possible. Without a proper phase lock, it would take at least thirty minutes, I said." A sigh. "And even that was probably an understatement. In fact, when . . ."

As Scott went on with his story, undaunted by the flagging attention of those around him, someone stuck a control padd in front of Geordi's face. He traced it to the engineer that was holding it out.

"Commander?" said Moreno, a petite brunette.

La Forge nodded and took the padd. "Thanks."

"You're welcome, sir," said Moreno, and stood there awaiting his reaction. As he studied the padd, trying valiantly to concentrate, Scott continued his story.

" 'Ye cannae change the laws of physics,' I said. But of course, he would nae listen. So we had to come up with a new engine start-up routine . . . easier said than done, considering the situation we . . ."

Finally, Geordi managed to focus on the padd. He grunted. "The alpha-band radiation is pretty high, isn't it?" Making a notation on the padd, he looked up at Moreno. "We should run a complete—"

Suddenly, he heard a loud, urgent voice: Captain Scott's. "Mr. La Forge! Do ye know that yer bloody dilithium crystals are about to fracture?"

The older man had moved off toward the warp core while Geordi was occupied with Moreno. Having opened the dilithium chamber at the center of the core, he was examining the dilithium crystals with a critical eye.

"Excuse me," he told Moreno, thrusting the padd back at her. Hurrying over to the warp core, he shut the chamber door, eliciting a startled look from Scott.

"Laddie!" the older man sputtered. "Do ye know what ye're—"

Geordi's patience was starting to wear thin. "We recomposite the crystals while they're still within the articulation frame," he explained, in a somewhat terser tone than he'd intended.

Scott's brow furrowed. He looked puzzled.

"Aye, lad . . . that would save a lot o' time. But how do you manage to—?"

That did it. Geordi had tried, he really had. But it was absolutely impossible to humor Scott and still get anything done.

"Mr. Scott," he said, *"please.* I'd like to explain everything, really. But the captain wants this spectrographic analysis done by thirteen hundred hours. So if you'll excuse me . . ."

With that, he turned his back on the older man and retreated into his office. Out of the corner of his eye, he saw Scott watching him for a moment. Then, uninvited, he went in and quietly moved to Geordi's side.

Is there no end to this? asked the chief engineer. No relief?

"Would ye mind . . . a little advice?" asked Scott.

Geordi decided he would mind. He didn't want any advice at all. But he held his tongue, hoping that once Scott gave it to him, he'd leave him alone.

"Starships' captains are like children," the man said in an avuncular tone. "They want everything right now and they want it their way. The secret is to give them what they need, not what they want."

Scott's attitude really pricked Geordi. Worse, the

advice itself went completely against the grain of his personality.

"I told him I'd have that analysis done in an hour," Geordi said firmly.

Scott grinned conspiratorially. "An' how long will it *really* take you?"

Geordi was puzzled now—genuinely puzzled. "An hour," he replied.

The other man seemed shocked. "Ye didnae tell him how long it was *really* going to take you?"

Geordi was irritated—and getting more so by the second. "Of course I did."

Scott rolled his eyes in mock disappointment. "Laddie, laddie, laddie. Ye've got a lot to learn if ye want them to think of ye as a miracle worker. Take it from me, ye've got to—"

Every man has his threshold, a line beyond which he can tolerate no more. Geordi had just reached his. He rounded on Scott.

"Look, sir," he said, "I've tried to be patient. I've tried to be polite. But I've got a job to do here—and you're getting in my way."

The last thing he expected was that Scott's own temper would flare . . . but flare it did. Every engineer in the place turned and stared as his voice rose, trembling with righteous emotion.

"I'll have ye know I was driving starships while your grandfather was still in diapers. I should think ye'd be *grateful* for a wee bit o' help—"

Geordi had had enough of this. It was embarrassing. It was stupid. And it had to be stopped before it went any further.

Rather than fan the flames any higher, he turned

away from Scott . . . just focused on his monitor and ignored the man. It was a mistake; Scott took it as an insult, and his voice waxed even louder for one last barrage.

"Then I'll leave ye to yer work, *Mr.* La Forge!"

With that, the man stormed out of engineering. Everyone watched him go. In his wake, there was an inescapable feeling that the whole thing could have been handled a lot better.

Geordi cursed under his breath. He was already sorry about the incident, damned sorry. But it was too late; the damage had been done.

Chapter Seven

NOT SO LONG AGO, Scott's quarters had seemed so spacious he didn't know what to do with them. Now they felt too small—like a cage, slowly but surely closing in on him—as he paced from one bulkhead to the other and back again.

"In the way," he muttered, not for the first time. "He actually said I was in the way!" He harrumphed loudly. "Used to be engineers had a wee bit o' respect for one another. Used to matter if a man spent his whole life in the bowels of a starship and never—"

Abruptly, the door chimed. Scott turned.

"What do ye want?" he demanded.

Scott wasn't sure what he'd expected, but it wasn't what he *got*. As the door slid aside, it revealed one of the loveliest women he'd ever had the pleasure to meet. The smile on her smooth-skinned face was so pleasant, so disarming, that he felt compelled to back away from his anger.

"Is this a bad time?" she asked, her large, dark eyes fairly dancing beneath a fringe of curly black hair.

"Uh . . . no," said Scott. He extended his hand to her. "Captain Montgomery Scott at your service. What can I do for you?"

She took his hand and grasped it firmly. "Deanna Troi, ship's counselor. And actually, I'm here to see if there's anything *I* can do for *you.*"

Scott didn't quite know what to make of that, but she was much too pretty to dismiss out of hand. Gesturing, he offered her a seat, then took one himself.

"I thank ye kindly for your concern, lass. But I'm set for now. The quarters are more than adequate. And the replicator is an honest-to-goodness wonder . . ."

Scott smiled at her. She smiled back. But he still didn't know why she was here. And maybe, he mused, he didn't care—as long as she stayed a while.

"I'm glad you're comfortable," said Troi. "But I was actually more interested in how you *feel.*"

For a brief moment, Scott had visions of something more than a friendly encounter. But he hadn't even met the woman until moments ago. And though he was still a handsome man, if he did say so himself, he just couldn't imagine . . .

"How I *feel?*" he repeated lamely.

"Yes," said Troi. "It would be perfectly normal to feel disoriented, confused or even frightened following the kind of experience you've just had."

Scott still didn't get it. "I suppose it's been . . . a mite bewilderin', yes."

There was an awkward pause as Scott tried to figure out where all this was headed. Troi straightened in her seat a bit, as if considering a different tack.

"I'm sure you have a lot of questions about what's happened over the last seventy-five years," she declared. "If you'd like, I can help you access some of our historical records . . . maybe help you discover what happened to your family . . . or friends."

Scott recoiled at the suggestion, surprising even himself. Family? Friends? "I dinnae think I'm ready for that just yet," he said. "It's a hard thing to come to grips with . . . I mean, the fact that everyone ye once knew is probably . . ."

His voice trailed off—as he suddenly realized what tone this conversation was taking. He looked at Troi with suspicion.

"Pardon me fer asking," he began, "but tell me, what exactly is a . . . ship's counselor?"

"I'm here to watch over the emotional well-being of our crew," she explained. And smiling that incredible, bonnie smile of hers, she added: "And of course, that of our guests as well."

Scott felt his eyes narrowing. "And ye're an officer?"

Troi nodded. "Yes. They started assigning counselors to starships about forty years ago, when they realized that the pressures of extended space travel—"

Scott's suspicions were confirmed. "Ye're a psychologist!" he said.

"Among other things," Troi responded, as calm and even-keeled as ever. "As I said, I'm here to make sure—"

Scott scowled. "La Forge sent ye here, didn't he? He did! I may be old, but I'm nae *crazy!*"

Troi shook her head. "You misunderstand, Captain Scott. Geordi didn't send me. And I know you're not crazy."

Scott got to his feet, annoyed at the whole affair. What had started out as something very pleasant was turning into just another form of humiliation. Hell, he was getting to be an *expert* at humiliation.

"Ye're damned right," he told her. "And since we're in agreement on that point, ye should know I dinnae need a ship's counselor, or a psychologist, or whatever else ye may be." He paused, feeling his cheeks grow hot. And in a voice that was so whisper-thin it surprised him, he said: "I know what I need—and it's nae *here."*

Nor would it ever be, as far as he could tell. The weight of that realization hit him with an almost physical impact.

For a moment, Troi looked as if she might try to convince him otherwise. Then she must have thought better of it, because she just rose from her seat and folded her arms across her chest.

"I hope you'll come to feel differently, Captain Scott. In the meantime, I'll be available if you decide you want to see me again."

Scott harrumphed. Not bloody likely, he mused, as he watched her exit his quarters and disappear behind the sliding door.

* * *

As Deanna Troi negotiated the corridor outside Scott's door, she felt the darkness inside her slowly dissipating. *Scott's* darkness. She sighed.

Such despair. She had seen men succumb to lesser burdens. She had seen the shadows of suffering eat them from within, until there was nothing left of them but hollow shells.

And yet, Scott did not seem to be in danger of that. He was carrying his load with remarkable fortitude, uncanny courage. Troi could not help but admire him for it.

Of course, it would have been better for him if he had opened up to her. She could have lightened his load, perhaps shown him a personal future he would not have thought possible.

Hope—that was her stock in trade. But he had not let her peddle it in his presence. The same courage that kept him sane in a strange environment would not let him accept what she had to offer.

Nor could she press her case. If Scott wanted her to intervene now, he would ask. Shaking her head, feeling a little defeated, she entered the turbolift and headed for the bridge.

Of all the nerve. Of all the bloody, condescending nerve.

To even suggest that he, Montgomery Scott, might need a psychologist—a blasted *headshrinker*. Hadn't he been through more harrowing experiences across the length and breadth of this galaxy than there were people on this twenty-fourth–century version of the *Enterprise?* And hadn't he managed to keep mind and body together through it all?

Scott didn't know exactly where he was going as he stalked along the corridor. What's more, he didn't care.

He just had to walk, to get his blood pumping. To figure things out.

If only he were back on his own *Enterprise*. Then he could have curled up in his quarters with a bottle of fine scotch and bit by bit gotten some perspective on what had happened to him . . . what was still happening to him.

Scott shook his head. Psychologist *indeed*. All he needed was a place of refuge where he could wet his whistle and mull it all over.

As he negotiated a curve in the corridor, he couldn't help but notice the looks he was getting from those who passed him going in the opposite direction. Did they know about him? Had they heard?

And were *they* going to offer him some advice too? Some twenty-fourth–century psychological gobble-dygoop?

Scott was so busy avoiding the gazes of the people in the corridor that he almost overlooked the one set of eyes that wasn't trained on him. If it wasn't for their color—a vibrant gold—and the pallor of the skin surrounding them, he would never have given them a second glance.

But he did. And what he saw piqued his curiosity enough for him to do an about-face and head the other way.

His initial assessment had been that the specimen in question was just an alien. A representative of a race that had joined the Federation sometime in the seventy-five years he'd been away. Then some sixth sense—the kind that made him the best ship's engineer in the fleet of his day—told him otherwise.

This was a mechanical man. An artificial life form. An *android*—or at least, that's what they had called them a century ago.

And it was wearing a Starfleet uniform—with a lieutenant's pips on the collar, no less. This . . . *construct* . . . was an officer on the *Enterprise*. First Klingons and now this!

Intrigued, Scott accelerated a bit and caught up with the android. Immediately, those golden eyes slid in his direction, taking him in.

"May I be of assistance?" it asked.

Scott chuckled. It even sounded artificial. Its speech pattern was too precise, too perfect . . . too devoid of emotion to have come from a living pair of vocal cords.

"May ye be of assistance?" the human echoed. Aye, he thought. Ye can assist me in twisting yer bloody head off, so I can get a peek down yer neck to see what makes ye tick.

But he didn't express that sentiment out loud. He didn't feel right speaking that way to a fellow officer, even if it was just a thing made of nuts and bolts.

The android tilted his head to one side. It was a subtle movement, but noticeable nonetheless. "You are Captain Scott," it observed.

So it knew him. But then, if it was an officer on this ship, it would have been its business to know such things.

"Right ye are," said Scott. "And who might you be?"

"My name is Data," it replied simply.

Data, eh? "An interesting name," the human observed.

"I am an android," it went on, as if it recognized that an explanation might be in order.

"I can see that," Scott told it. "I've seen my share of androids before, y'know. Back at Exo Three, we had one that looked like our captain sitting in the command chair. And then there was the pack that Harry Mudd unleashed on us, though before long he wished he had never considered it. And of course, there was that poor, sweet thing on Holberg Nine-One-Seven-G . . . I dinnae suppose I need to go on."

Data nodded. "Nonetheless, you did not expect to see an android serving as an officer on the *Enterprise.* Correct?"

Scott looked at him. Perceptive, wasn't he? Had he been that obvious about it? Or had Data just drawn a logical conclusion from the information at hand?

"Something like that," the human admitted. "So . . . how *did* ye come to be an officer here? Were ye built for the purpose?" Another question occurred to him. "Does every ship have an android aboard it these days?"

It was a chilling thought, Scott mused. Machines had no business being in charge of starships. They'd proven that a hundred years go, the time Starfleet inflicted the M-5 unit on them.

"I am the only android presently serving in Starfleet," Data responded. "Nor was I created to do so. I was originally designed and built by Dr. Noonian Soong, a cyberneticist, who had no idea that I would one day become an officer on a starship. As for my joining the *Enterprise* . . . my career path was not unusual. Like anyone else, I first attended Starfleet Academy and served in lesser capacities on various other vessels."

The human nodded. There was something strangely *likeable* about this mechanical man. He was so forthcoming, so honest. So downright . . . friendly. And no doubt, an excellent source of information. After all, his name was *Data,* wasn't it?

I can use a source of information, Scott told himself. Especially one who doesn't seem to mind my asking a bunch of questions—unlike that upstart La Forge.

And he still had *lots* of questions. About the warp engines, the transporter units, the phaser banks, the sensor array . . . and of course, about Data himself.

Scott put his hand on the android's shoulder. "I'd like to speak with ye sometime at greater length," he said. "I dinnae suppose ye'll be getting off duty soon, eh?"

"As a matter of fact," Data told him, "I am off-duty right now."

A stroke of luck—one of the few Scott had had since boarding this ship. "Are ye now? Splendid. Then maybe there's some place we can chew the fat a bit."

The android looked at him, his golden eyes narrowing ever so slightly. Then, abruptly, he seemed to understand.

"Chew the fat," he repeated. "Converse. Engage in discussion." A pause. "I would like that," he concluded. "And I believe I have an appropriate venue in mind. It is called Ten-Forward."

"Wherever ye like, laddie," said Scott. He'd never heard of Ten-Forward; it was probably a lab of some kind. But then, that didn't really matter, did it? After all, they were going there to exchange information, not to swap tall tales over a bottle of Saurian brandy.

Data had barely escorted Captain Scott into the Ten-Forward lounge when he knew he had made the right decision. It was obvious from the man's broad grin and the way he rubbed his hands together that Scott felt right at home here.

"Why did ye nae tell me ye had a tavern on board?" he asked the android.

Data looked at him. "You did not ask," he replied.

That brought a flood of laughter from Scott. "Ah, Mr. Data, I had my doubts about ye, I must admit— but ye're nothing like the androids I used to know." He slapped Data on the back. "Lay on, Macduff."

The android looked at him. It took his positronic brain a moment to find the reference. And even after it had, he didn't quite grasp the connection.

"Macduff was a character in William Shakespeare's *Macbeth*," he noted. "What does that have to do with—"

"It's only an expression, lad, only an expression. Here now, that looks like the bar. What do ye say we belly up to it?" And without waiting for an answer, he took the second officer by the arm and pulled him in the necessary direction.

As they sat down on neighboring stools, a waiter came over to them. "May I help you, sir?" he asked Scott, who was nearer to him.

"Aye, lad. Scotch. Neat."

"And you, sir?" the waiter asked Data.

"I will have the same," the android replied.

Scott gazed at him with new admiration. "Thatta boy, Mr. Data—though I would nae have figured ye fer a scotch man."

"I am not a scotch man," the android told him. "In fact, this is the first time I have ever placed such an order."

"Is that so?" said Scott. "Well, then, ye're in fer a most pleasant surprise." He paused. "Unless, of course, alcohol does nae agree with ye." Then he rolled his eyes and chuckled. "What am I thinking? If it did nae agree with ye, ye would nae have brought me here, now would ye?"

As Data puzzled over Captain Scott's remarks, the waiter brought them their drinks. Scotch was an amber-colored beverage, the android noted. And as his companion requested, it had been served without ice in short, squat glasses.

"Thank ye, lad," said Scott, eyeing his liquid portion with obvious fondness. "I'm forever indebted to ye. Bottoms—"

Suddenly, with the glass halfway to his lips, he noticed something amiss—or at least, it seemed that way to Data. For a moment, he held his drink up to the light and inspected it.

Perhaps it was not the quality of scotch the man was accustomed to, the android surmised. In any case, Scott didn't carry on his inspection for very long. Shrugging, he turned to Data.

"Oh well," he said. "Any port in a storm, eh?" And his doubts apparently overcome, he took a hearty gulp of the stuff.

The android did the same. But he'd barely swallowed when he heard the sound of something hard striking the surface of the bar.

"Are ye trying to poison me?" Scott demanded. There was a look of disgust on his face as he wiped his mouth with the back of his hand. "What in blazes *is* this?"

The waiter was by their side in record time. "Is something wrong?" he asked.

"I'll say something's wrong," the older man spat. "Ye did nae bring me what I asked for."

"Didn't you order scotch?" asked the plainly confused waiter.

"That I did," said Scott, thrusting the glass back into the man's hand.

The waiter looked at the glass. "But . . . but that's what I brought you, sir. Scotch."

Scott leaned close to the man and said, in a voice taut with frustration: "Laddie, I was drinkin' scotch about a hundred years before ye were born, and I can tell ye one thing fer certain: whatever *this* is, it is most definitely *not* scotch."

The waiter was at a loss. He just stood there for a moment, baffled.

But Data had figured it out. "I believe I may be of some assistance," he offered. "You see, Captain Scott is unaware of the existence of synthehol."

The older man turned to him. "Synthehol?" he asked, making it sound like a curse. "What the bleedin' blazes is that?"

"It is an alcohol substitute," said the android. "Synthehol simulates the appearance, smell and

117

taste of alcohol, but its intoxicating effects can be dismissed in humanoids with a mental effort. Therefore, one may imbibe to one's heart's content—without suffering any negative consequences afterward. Though it was originally developed by the Ferengi, it is now served aboard all Federation starships."

Scott just looked at him. He did not seem happy.

"Synthehol," he echoed.

"That is correct," Data responded.

"And the Ferengi . . . ?" he started to ask—but quickly erased the question with a wave of his hand. "No, dinnae tell me. I dinnae want to know."

The android answered him anyway. "The Ferengi Alliance is made up of a number of planetary systems with a centralized government. The Ferengi themselves are intergalactic traders whose main motivation is profit. In appearance, they are quite short, dark, highly energetic humanoids with exceedingly large . . ."

"Mr. Data!" cried Scott. "I said I did *nae* want to know!"

". . . ears," the android finished, and was still. Obviously, the human's statement had been meant literally rather than colloquially.

Scott sighed. "Synthetic scotch and synthetic commanders. I'm beginning t' *hate* the twenty-fourth century," he said with passionate sincerity.

"I'm sorry to hear that," replied a feminine voice. Data and his companion turned at the same time, tracing the voice to its source.

"Guinan," declared the android.

"In the flesh," she said. And then to Captain Scott: "I don't believe we've been introduced. You are . . . ?"

"Montgomery Scott," the human answered—a bit wearily, Data thought.

"Nice to meet you, Montgomery Scott. Say . . . aren't you the fellow they fished out of the *Jenolen?*"

He nodded. "One and the same, lass. Though I'm beginnin' to wonder if it was worth it."

Guinan smiled placidly. "I don't think you mean that, Montgomery Scott. I think you've been saying a lot of things you don't mean."

Scott looked at her, narrow-eyed. "Dinnae tell me ye're another of those *counselors.*" He uttered the word as if it left a bad taste in his mouth.

She shook her head. "Nope. I'm not one of those. I'm the person who runs *this* place." She indicated Ten-Forward with a sweep of her arm.

The man's eyes lit up with indignation. "I see. Then you're the one responsible for serving that synthewhoozis instead of real scotch."

Guinan shrugged. "I've never had any complaints before."

"Well," Scott told her, "ye've got one now. Let me tell ye something, Lassie. I was drinkin' scotch about a hundred years before ye were born—"

"I doubt it," she replied.

He looked at her disbelievingly. "I beg your pardon?"

"You *weren't* drinking scotch a hundred years before I was born," she corrected. "And for that matter, neither was your great-great-grandfather. But of course, that's another story entirely."

Scott considered her for a moment or two and then turned to Data. "Is she on the level?"

The android nodded. "I have seen firsthand evidence of her veracity."

"True," said Guinan, drawing the human's attention again, and Data's as well. "In any case, Captain Scott, since you don't care for what we're serving here . . ."

Walking around to the back of the bar, she bent down and reached for something. When she came up again, she had a very old, dusty bottle full of a green liquid. Blowing on it, she dislodged a considerable amount of dust. Then, with something of a flourish, she placed it next to a clean glass on the bar's polished surface.

Scott's eyes asked a question. Guinan answered it.

"I keep a . . . shall we say . . . *limited* supply of nonsyntheholic beverages behind the bar. Perhaps this one will be more to your liking, Captain."

Data tried to read the label, but he was unable to. It had faded too badly from the effects of age and spillage.

Scott looked at the bottle, then at Guinan, and then back to the bottle again. Curious, Data picked it up, removed the cap and sniffed the contents.

"What is it?" asked the human.

Data told Scott the only thing he knew for certain. "It is green," he said.

Scott eyed the bottle again and shrugged. "Well," he declared, "I guess that's good enough fer me."

Data could hardly disagree with the observation. Turning the bottle over to Scott, he watched the man pour himself two fingers' worth. Then he raised his glass and saluted Guinan and the android.

"Cheers," Scott said. And then, with something of a make-do expression on his face, he drank.

Chapter Eight

IN A CORRIDOR, Scott was standing just outside the doors of a holodeck. He was still carrying the bottle of green liquor and the glass from Ten-Forward, and he was more than a little drunk. He activated the bulkhead computer terminal.

"Please enter program," said the computer's smooth, synthetic voice.

"The android at the bar told me ye could show me my old ship. So lemme see the old girl."

"Insufficient data. Please quantify parameters."

"The *Enterprise*. Show me the bridge of the *Enterprise*, ye chattering piece of—"

"There have been five Federation ships with that name," the computer informed him. "Please specify by registry number."

Scott cursed beneath his breath. "NCC-One-Seven-Oh-One. No bloody A, B, C or D!"

"Program complete," the computer announced softly. "Enter when ready."

Scott took a step toward the strange interlocking doors of the holodeck—and then stopped. What was holding him back?

The possibility that the fantasy wouldn't live up to the reality? Some vague, superstitious fear of waking the dead—for the *Enterprise*-no-suffix was certainly that. He knew; he'd seen her die with his own eyes.

"Ah, blast," he said to no one in particular. "Faint heart never won fair lady." And with that, he stepped forward again.

The doors parted. And a moment later, as if by magic, Scotty found himself on the bridge of his old ship. *Kirk*'s old ship. All the monitors were blinking and flashing and the sound of the old scanners filled the air.

For a second or two, as he moved to a spot beside the captain's chair, Scott felt as if he'd come home. Going over to his old station, just to one side of the turbolift, he turned and took a look around.

And was unexpectedly depressed. There was nobody here. Nobody at all. It didn't seem right to be alone on a place that was once such a hive of activity.

Without his old friends manning the consoles and stations, without Spock and McCoy exchanging barbs and the captain laughing up his sleeve at them, the *Enterprise* was like a ghost ship. The Flying Dutchman, Scott thought.

No. The Flying Scotsman, he amended. Doomed to wander the universe in perpetuity, no longer wanted, no longer needed.

Like Scott himself. He heaved a sigh.

Damn. He hadn't come here to hold a wake for himself. He'd come to remind himself of a time when he *was* wanted and needed.

Scott poured himself a stiff drink, trying to shake his feelings of melancholy. Lifting his glass, he saluted the people who weren't there.

"Here's to ye, lads," he intoned, as if at a wake. He drank down the libation.

And then he realized . . . this holodeck could recreate a lot more than places and things, if he'd understood correctly. It could recreate *people* as well.

"Computer," he said, "I need some company here. Some familiar faces."

"Please specify," came the response.

He chuckled and straightened in his seat. "Captain James T. Kirk. First Officer Spock. Chief Medical Officer Leonard McCoy."

It felt good just to say their names. It seemed to give them a reality even before the holodeck worked its magic.

"Lieutenant Sulu at the helm, Ensign Chekov at navigation. And at communications, the loveliest lass who ever wore a uniform—Lieutenant Uhura."

"Mission-tape information on all these individuals is on file. Please select a time frame."

Ah, of course. A time frame. People weren't like the bridge of a starship. They changed slightly from year to year, from month to month, even from day to day. He thought for a moment.

It had to be at least a third of the way into the original five-year mission—or Chekov wouldn't have been there yet. And he *wanted* Chekov there. Of all those who'd sat at the navigation station—DeSalle,

Bailey, Stiles and on and on—Chekov was the one with whom Scott had been the closest.

"Let's see," he said, scratching his jaw.

How about just after that tribbles business? He smiled despite himself, recalling those furry little creatures and all the trouble they'd caused. Not that he'd minded the trouble all that much. It had given him a chance to mix it up with the Klingons, to let off a little steam . . .

Those were the days, all right. Those were the bloody days.

Too bad that sort of thing couldn't happen anymore. Now that the Klingons and the Federation were allies, there would be no more brawling between them. No more knockdown-dragouts with the horny-headed barbarians, no more defending the honor of the *Enterprise* and the fleet.

Too bad, Scott mused. Another valuable cultural phenomenon lost to the ravages of time.

He felt the tug of the silence around him. It seemed to cry out for relief. For *voices.*

"I know, I know," he said. "Ye're waiting."

The computer had no reply, but its impatience was almost palpable. All right then. A time frame. Hmmm . . .

Then it hit him. Of course. Why hadn't he thought of it before?

"Stardate 4534.7," he told the computer. "And as far as my friends are concerned, I'm to look now as I did then. Understood?"

"Processing," the machine replied.

A second later, Scott had company. It hadn't exactly *appeared*—at least, not in the way he'd expected. It was just *there*, as if it had been sitting or standing on the bridge all along.

He muttered an oath. They were there. They were really there. All his friends, in the places where he'd always thought of them. All except Dr. McCoy, and he'd no doubt be along presently.

"How much longer, Mr. Sulu?" asked the figure in the center seat.

"We're right on time, Captain," replied the helmsman. "We'll be in docking range of Starbase Nine in two hours, twenty-five minutes and thirty seconds."

"Excellent, Lieutenant. We can all use the rest, after that business back on Triskelion. And nobody makes steak au poivre like Commander Tattinger."

The navigator turned to peer back at the captain. "Steak au poivre is actually a Russian dish, sair. My mother made it for us vhen ve vere growing up. Vith just a pinch of paprika."

The figure in the center seat cleared his throat. "I see, Mr. Chekov. I'll have to remember to share that with the commander."

Training his gaze on the command chair, Scott leaned forward. "Captain Kirk?" he ventured.

The captain turned and rose to face his chief engineer. He looked young, vital. Brash, in a way that Scott had all but forgotten. It seemed the holodeck had remembered Kirk better than his old colleague had.

There was something wrong with that, wasn't there? With a machine remembering a man better than that man's friend?

"Yes, Scotty," said Kirk. "Is something . . . ?"

Suddenly, he stopped in mid-question, his gaze

going to the bottle in Scott's hand. He looked up until their eyes met. "Mr. Scott," he said firmly but calmly, "what in the name of sanity are you doing here with that bottle?"

What indeed! "Stop program," Scott commanded.

The program froze, but Kirk's eyes still reproached him. Scott put the bottle and the glass down on the deck beside him.

"Computer," he said, "can ye hide these for me?" He pointed to the items in question.

Abruptly, they were gone. Vanished into thin air.

"Good. Now resume the program."

As life came back to Kirk, he blinked. "That's strange," he said.

"What is, sir?" asked Scott.

The captain shook his head. "For a second there, I thought I saw . . ."

"A bottle," Scott reminded him. "Ye said something about a *bottle,* sir."

Kirk's eyes narrowed. "I could have sworn . . ."

"Aye, sir?"

The captain frowned. "Never mind, Scotty." His demeanor changed, becoming more businesslike. "Have you run those diagnostics on the warp engines?"

"I have indeed, sir," said Scott. And he had, too— about a hundred years ago. "They're runnin' as smooth as Saurian brandy."

Kirk tilted his head to one side, his eyes narrowing. Probably thinking again about the bottle. "An interesting analogy," he noted.

Scott nodded. "Thank ye, sir."

Pulling down on the front of his tunic, the captain

surveyed his bridge. Funny, thought Scott. Their uniforms looked a little skimpy to his eye. Had the computer erred, or had they always looked that way?

Spock, who had been hovering over his science monitor, chose that moment to straighten and turn to the captain. "Sir?"

"Yes, Mr. Spock?"

The Vulcan's features were even more severe than in Scott's memories, his demeanor more cold and aloof—more *alien*. "Sensors indicate a rather unusual phenomenon off the starboard bow. According to my files, we have encountered such a phenomenon before, but never one of such magnitude."

Kirk grunted. "Does this phenomenon have a name, Spock?"

"It does," said the first officer. "However, I believe you will recognize it without any help from me."

With that, Spock turned to his control board and made the requisite adjustments to project his finding onto the main viewer. All eyes turned to the large screen, awaiting their first inkling of what Spock was talking about.

Scott knew what it would be, naturally. For him, this was déjà vu. But he didn't let on that he knew—it would have spoiled the surprise.

Even before the new image came up on the viewscreen, Chekov was chuckling into his fist, unable to quite contain himself. Finally, they all got to see the phenomenon.

It was a snakelike mass of iridescent energies, writhing in and out of every color imaginable. And it spelled out a single message: "Happy Anniversary, Scotty!"

His anniversary with Starfleet, that is. A recognition of a romance that had begun the first time he set foot in Chris Pike's engineering room.

Right on cue, the turbolift doors opened wide, allowing McCoy to come in carrying a big, white cake with a bonnie tartan design on top of it. "I hope you all like it," he said. "After all, I'm a doctor, not a baker."

Scott allowed his jaw to drop. "Of all the . . . !"

He looked around, at Kirk and Spock and then at all the others, accusing them with mock intensity. They were grinning like people who'd kept a secret about as long as they possibly could.

All except for Spock, of course. But then, he was smiling too. He was just doing it on the inside.

"What a pack of bloody actors!" he exclaimed, and their smiles widened even more. "An' how long have ye been planning this?"

Kirk shrugged, stealing a conspiratory glance at McCoy. "Not very long," he said. "Only since about your *last* anniversary."

Scott looked at the first officer. "An' how did they corral ye into this, Mr. Spock? I thought Vulcans didnae *know* how to deceive."

Spock cocked an eyebrow. "We know how," he explained simply. "We simply choose not to—unless there is no other option." He cast a withering glance about the bridge. "And believe me," he told Scott, completely deadpan, "on this occasion, there was no other option left open to me."

That brought peals of laughter from all assembled. And before they died down, Uhura had come over from her communications station.

She put an arm around Scott and gave him a kiss on the cheek. "Many happy returns Scotty," she told him, her breath as sweet as toffee.

Scott could feel his face burning with embarrassment, just as it had burned the first time she'd graced him with that celebratory kiss. Fondly, he recalled another time Uhura had wanted to kiss him—and in an entirely different way.

"Thank ye, lass," he told her. "That was the best gift of all."

"Thanks a lot," said Sulu. "And what are *we?* Dim sum?"

"That's right," Chekov chimed in. "You think it vas easy to program the viewscreen to do that? Especially vithout tipping you off?"

Scott conceded their points. "I thank ye all," he said. "For this." He indicated the splendidly wrought message on the viewer. "And for being the best friends a man could wish for."

Kirk nodded approvingly. "Well said, Mr. Scott."

"Indeed," said McCoy. "And now, before this gets any more maudlin than it has already, I think it's high time we had some cake."

In the course of the high time that followed, little of that cake was consumed—much to the chief medical officer's chagrin. As it turned out, McCoy was right. He *was* a doctor and not a baker.

But that didn't stop any of them from having a good time. So good a time, in fact, that Montgomery Scott would remember it fondly for the rest of his life. And then, just as the party wound down so they could devote their attention to docking at Starbase Nine, Jim Kirk escorted him back to his bridge station.

"Scotty . . ." the captain began.

"Aye, sir?" Scott responded, taking his seat. He couldn't remember exactly what Kirk had said to him at this point, but he looked forward to hearing it again. After all, the captain was one of the brightest men Scott had ever had the honor to know.

"Scotty," Kirk began again. "About that bottle . . ."

Before the captain could finish his thought, he suddenly froze in place—as the holodeck doors opened and admitted another starship captain. A captain of the *Enterprise*, in fact. However, this one was in command of the *Enterprise*, known by the suffix D.

As the doors swooshed closed behind him, Picard looked around at the bridge and its occupants. Then he turned to Scott and smiled apologetically.

"I hope I'm not interrupting," said the captain. "I was just coming off-duty and I wanted to see how you were doing."

"No problem at all," said Scott. He indicated his former comrades with a sweep of his arm. "These are the men and women I used to serve with."

Picard nodded. "Yes. I surmised as much." His gaze seemed to fix on Jim Kirk. "And that was your captain, I take it?"

The older man nodded. "He was indeed. James T. Kirk. I hope ye've heard of him—'cos if nae, there's something very wrong with yer history tapes."

Picard smiled. "I *have* heard of James Kirk . . . even before I took charge of the Enterprise." Steely-eyed, he appraised the captain—even as Kirk seemed to return the scrutiny. "Though somehow," Picard continued, "I always pictured him as being somewhat taller."

Scott grunted, instinctively leaping to his friend's defense. "He was big enough to blaze a trail from Earth to the limits of the galaxy, I can tell ye *that.*"

Again, Picard smiled. Not Kirk's boyish smile, but one that disarmed its subject just as effectively.

"I'm certain he was, Captain Scott. It was not my intention to imply otherwise." For a moment longer, Picard sized up his predecessor of a century earlier, perhaps remembering tales told of the legendary Kirk in his Academy classes or in some officers' lounge.

These two captains were different men, Scott noted. Even frozen in this casual moment, Kirk was somehow more dynamic, more reckless, more willing to take chances—charged with the kind of energy that was needed to tame a wild frontier. And Picard? Picard was calculation and control, a man who seemed more at ease with the great responsibility of commanding a starship. A man with the skill to guide his vessel through the most bizarre of alien dangers.

They were different men, all right. But then, they were the products of different times. In Kirk's era, the galaxy was wide open, rife with danger and filled with those who would enslave or exploit lesser beings. In Picard's era—now Scott's as well, whether he liked it or not—things seemed to be more complicated. From what he could tell, the dangers were fewer, but the need for a strong hand on the tiller was no less.

Turning to Scott, Picard tilted his head toward Jim Kirk and asked: "May I?"

It took the older man a second or two to understand

the request. But once he did, he had no objections. "Go right ahead," he said.

Picard looked up. "Computer . . . I will assume the role of a visiting captain—here to survey the bridge at Captain Kirk's invitation. None of the personalities in this program are to see my presence here or my garb as anything unusual."

"Program altered accordingly," came the response.

"Excellent," said Picard. He turned to Kirk again. "Resume program."

A heartbeat later, the bridge came alive again. Jim Kirk's eyes narrowed slightly as he took in the sight of Picard—this time, for real. Or at least, as real as it got in this dream-box of a holodeck.

"Captain," said Kirk. He grinned. "I'm glad you could make the celebration after all."

Picard smiled back. "I would not have missed it for the world." He looked around. "Though I must admit, I find it a trifle unsettling to participate in a party on the bridge of a starship."

"Well," said Kirk, "sometimes you've got to break the rules. After all," he went on, "these people have worked long and hard on this voyage. They've risked their lives for me." He glanced at Scott. "This man probably more often than any other. A celebration like this is the least I could do for him."

Scott smiled. "Thank ye, sir. Ye're too kind."

"Captain?" called Spock from his science station.

Two heads—Kirk's and Picard's—turned simultaneously. "Yes, Spock?" replied the captain who was in charge here.

"Sir," said the Vulcan, "we must prepare for our

approach to the starbase—which we will reach in . . ." He glanced at his monitor. "Exactly twenty-two minutes and nine seconds."

"Of course," said Kirk, taking his guest's arm and ushering him in Spock's direction. "But first, I'd like to introduce you to Captain Jean-Luc Picard. Captain Picard, this is Mr. Spock, my first officer."

As Scott looked on, Picard and the Vulcan exchanged deferential nods. "A pleasure to meet you, Mister Spock," said the captain of the *Enterprise*-D.

The first officer's brow creased ever so slightly. "Sir . . . do I know you? There is something about you that seems . . ." He paused, somewhat discomfited. "Familiar," he finished—rather lamely, Scott thought.

Picard shook his head. "No. You have never seen me before this moment," he assured Spock. "But I feel as if I know you nonetheless. Let us just say . . . that your reputation precedes you."

There was something more there than met the eye, Scott decided. After all, Picard had purposely avoided answering Spock's question in the manner it had been posed. What's more, the Vulcan seemed aware of it, though he was too polite to pursue the matter any further.

"I am . . . honored," said Spock.

"You have served the Federation in good stead. And I fully expect you will continue to do so."

That cinched it. Somewhere along the line, Picard *had* met Spock . . . the *real* Spock, not just a holodeck recreation of him.

Nor was there any reason he should not have.

Vulcans were notoriously long-lived, and even in this era Spock would have been far from elderly.

Spock . . . *alive.* It was a cheering thought. But it led to other thoughts a whole lot less cheering, for that was probably not the case with some of Scott's other comrades. He looked around the bridge again and saw them all in a new light.

Kirk, Spock and McCoy. Uhura, Sulu and Chekov. How many had survived, and in what shape? Who had lived to see this day of optical data chips and five-phase autocontainment fields . . . and who had not?

Out of the corner of his eye, Scott noticed a reflection—his reflection—in one of the monitor screens of his engineering station. Turning toward it, he studied his image there.

It wasn't like Kirk's or McCoy's or Uhura's. It wasn't young. It was old. Ancient, it seemed to him. He didn't belong in this kind of company anymore. And they didn't belong here, on a ship that none of them would have recognized as their beloved *Enterprise.*

Suddenly finding that he had lost his taste for this particular program, Scott called out. "Computer, delete these people."

Instantly, faster than his mind could register the fact, they were absent from the program. There was no one on the bridge besides Scott and Picard.

The captain turned to him, his eyes framing a question. The older man shrugged. "It was time," he said. Then he remembered something else.

"I'd like my refreshments to reappear," he told the computer.

Before he knew it, his bottle of green liquor and its accompanying glass had assumed a visible reality again. Stooping to pick them up, he held them out meaningfully to Picard.

"Have a drink with me, Captain?"

For a moment, Picard gazed at the bottle full of green liquid, as if weighing his tolerance for it. "Why not?" he said finally.

Pouring a drink from the bottle, Scott handed it to the captain. The contents caught the light and shimmered as they sloshed.

"I got it in yer Ten-Forward lounge," the older man explained. "I'm nae sure what it is, exactly, but I'd be careful with it if I were you. It has a real . . ."

Scott's voice trailed off as Picard suddenly threw back the drink in a single, fluid motion. Nor did it have the effect Scott expected. On the contrary, Picard didn't appear to be staggered in the slightest.

"Aldebaran whiskey," said the captain appreciatively, as he returned the glass. "Northern continent. Stardate 36455—a good year. Not too much rain."

Scott must have been open-mouthed, because Picard smiled at his expression. "Tell me something, Captain Scott. Who do you think gave that bottle to Guinan in the first place?"

Scott felt the laughter bubble up inside him, and he had no reason not to let it out. Lord knew, he'd done little in the way of laughing since he left the twenty-third century behind.

"Ye're full o' surprises, Captain Picard."

Picard shrugged. "I try not to be too predictable. Keeps my people on their toes." A pause. "No, that's a lie. I'm *very* predictable."

He took another look at the antiquated bridge. Since there was no longer anyone on it, the captain had to be attending to the technical details.

"Constitution-class," he announced at last.

"Aye," said Scott. "Ye're familiar with it?"

"There's one at the fleet museum," the captain replied. "Well-preserved, too." And then: "This is your *Enterprise?*"

Scott nodded thoughtfully. "One o' them. I actually served on two ships with that proud name. This was the first, though, the one I spent the most time aboard. She was also the first ship I ever served on as engineer."

Picard sat down at the next bridge station over from the engineering console. It was a gesture that said: tell me more.

Scott leaned toward him conspiratorially. "Ye know," said the older man, "I shipped out aboard eleven vessels in my career. Freighters, cruisers, starships, ye name it. But this is the only one I ever think about . . . the only one I ever really miss. Funny thing, is it nae?"

"Funny thing," Picard agreed. He looked up. "Computer, another glass. One like Captain Scott's."

Instantly, there was a glass in the captain's hand. He extended it meaningfully toward Scott.

"There ye go," said the older man, filling it and then his own. This time, they tossed back their drinks together.

"Ahh," said Scott, feeling it warm his insides on its way down.

For a time, there was an easy silence between them, a silence that made no demands on anyone. Nor was it a complete silence at that; in the background, there was the low base thrum of the old *Enterprise*'s various systems.

Running at peak efficiency—of course. Scott wouldn't have tolerated anything less.

Finally, he broke the silence. Turning to Picard, he asked: "What was the first ship *you* ever served on? As captain, I mean?"

Picard grunted. "It was called . . . the *Stargazer.*"

"Ye say it like an incantation," the older man noted.

The captain smiled. "There was nothing magical about it, I assure you. The *Stargazer* was an over-worked, underpowered vessel that was always on the verge of flying apart at the seams. In every measurable way, my *Enterprise* is a superior ship." A pause. "And yet, there are times when I miss that cramped little bridge more than I care to say."

Scott beamed. Here was a man who was very much like him, who could understand what he was going through.

"It's like the first time ye fall in love," he told Picard. "Ye dinnae ever love a woman quite the way ye did that first one. Here, allow me."

Scott poured another shot into the captain's glass. As before, the liquid gleamed as it captured the light. Then he poured himself a refill as well.

"A toast," he suggested. "To the *Enterprise* and the *Stargazer* . . . old girlfriends we'll never see again."

Clinking glasses, they drank up. Drawing a satisfied breath, Picard turned again to his companion. "And while we're on the subject of ships . . . what do you think of the *Enterprise*-D?"

"Ah," said Scott, "she's a beauty fer certain. A

dream in duranium. With a good crew, too, as far as I can tell."

Picard could hear the reservation in his voice. "But?"

Scott took in the bridge with a sweep of his arm. "When I was *here,*" he said, "I could tell ye the speed we were travelin' by the wee shiverin' in the deck plates. I could feel it when we came about, and tell ye our heading without even looking. On yer ship . . ." He shook his head. "Half the time, I cannae seem to tell up from down."

Suddenly, Scott was enveloped by a great sense of sadness, of loss. He turned again to his monitor screen and regarded his image there.

He was old. And like the comrades he had recreated moments earlier, he was out of place here, a round peg in a square hole. Time had passed him by—like a dinosaur, like a relic of some prehistoric age.

Maybe it would have been better if he'd been lost in the transporter like poor Franklin. Then he'd have gone out at the top of his game. He'd have been remembered for what he was, not as some pathetic has-been.

Picard put a hand on his shoulder. "Feeling a little disoriented?" he asked congenially.

Scott sighed. "Feeling *wrong,*" he replied. "I'm in the way here, Captain Picard. I'm a nuisance. Nothing's what it should be . . . where it should be. Damn! I feel so bloody . . . *useless.*"

Picard looked at him sympathetically. "Seventy-five years is a long time, my friend. A big gap. You shouldn't expect to close it in a day. If you'd like to study some of the technical—"

Scott shook his head peremptorily. "I'm nae eighteen, Captain. I cannae start over again like a raw cadet."

"You need not start over," Picard told him. "Not entirely."

The older man shook his head. Getting unsteadily to his feet, he moved toward the captain's chair, then turned back toward Picard.

"There comes a time," he said, "when a man finds he cannae fall in love again . . . when he knows that it's time to stop." Another wistful look around. "I dinnae belong on your ship, Captain. I belong on *this* one. This was my home. This was where I had a purpose. But this . . ." He used his glass to indicate the entirety of the bridge. ". . . is nae real. It's just a computer-generated fantasy. And I'm just an old man, living in his memories of days gone by."

For a moment, Picard looked as if he was going to continue to argue otherwise. But he didn't. He just sat there.

Looking up at the computer grid somewhere above him, Scott called: "Computer—shut this bloody thing off. It's time—high time—I acted my age."

Instantly, the old bridge vanished, leaving the two men on the stark, empty holodeck. Scott harrumphed at the sight of the yellow-on-black grid.

So this was what a dream looked like after all the trappings were stripped away. Somehow, it made him feel even emptier inside than before.

He nodded to Picard. Picard nodded back. And without another word, Montgomery Scott headed for the exit.

Chapter Nine

As Sousa entered the rec, he saw Kane sitting all alone. Tranh and the others were there too, but at the opposite end of the room.

That didn't seem right, somehow. Kane belonged with the group, in the middle of the conversation. After all, he was their unofficial leader. He was the one about whom everyone else revolved.

"Andy!" said Tranh, beckoning to Sousa. "Come on, have a seat."

Kane looked up for a moment and took note. Then he turned away again.

Sousa went over to the group and sat down, but he couldn't help glancing in Kane's direction. "What's going on?" he asked. "Why's Kane over there all by himself?"

Tranh shrugged. "It's his choice, no one else's. We

asked him to join us, but he refused." And then, in a lower voice: "If you ask me, he's embarrassed. After all that hype about being in tight with the captain, he's still getting the worst assignments imaginable."

"That's not his fault," Sousa countered.

"No one said it was," replied Tranh. "Personally, I sympathize with him. But I don't think he wants any of my sympathy."

Sousa made a decision. "Excuse me," he said. And getting up, he crossed the room to where Kane was sitting.

His fellow ensign looked up. He didn't seem any different. He still had that air of confidence about him—that bravado that had made Sousa envy him so. Hell, he *still* envied him, despite the fact that Kane's fortunes had taken a turn for the worse.

"Hey," he said. "Mind if I sit down?"

Kane shrugged. "Suit yourself, helm-jockey."

Sousa sat. "How are things down in the shuttlebay?" he asked.

His friend smiled—but it wasn't his usual grin. It didn't have that old Kane charm in it. Instead, it seemed brassy, fake, as if Kane was hiding something behind it. Something he didn't dare allow anyone else to see.

"They're fine, just fine. How are things up on the bridge?"

Sousa shrugged. "I've got no complaints."

Kane grunted. "Of course you don't." A pause. "That's the problem with you. You've got no ambition. You think you've gotten to the bridge, you've made it." His expression turned sour. "But it's a long race, y'know? And the winner isn't always the one who starts off the fastest."

Sousa shook his head. "I'm not racing with you, Kane. You're my friend." He leaned closer. "If you're hurting, I'm hurting. If you're angry about how they're treating you, I'm angry too."

The other man looked at him for a second or two. Then he started to laugh. It was a cutting kind of laughter, intended to hurt. And it did.

"That's good, Sousa. Like I really believe that. Like you really care what happens to the competition."

Sousa frowned. "Listen, man. I know what you're feeling. You're down. You're disappointed. But that's not going to last forever, okay?"

Kane chuckled derisively. "You've got it wrong, buddy. Very wrong. I'm not down and I'm not disappointed." He stood up. "I'm Darrin Kane. And I don't need you or anybody else. Got it?"

Suddenly, Sousa was angry. Here he'd tried to help the poor bastard—and look what he was getting for his trouble.

He stood, too. "You know, Kane, I used to think you were really something. But you want to prove me wrong, that's fine. You sit here in the corner and feel sorry for yourself. But don't think I don't see through you. Don't think there's *anyone* here who doesn't see through you."

Kane's mouth twisted then and he reached out to grab Sousa's tunic. But Sousa was too fast for him; he grabbed Kane's wrist instead.

And it might have gone farther than that, except there was a crowd of crew members around them before he knew it, and some of them were driving a wedge between him and Kane. They glared at each other across the wedge, too, as if they still wanted to go at it. But it was over.

"Come on," someone whispered in Sousa's ear. "Walk away, man, walk away—before this goes on somebody's record."

Sousa walked away. Not immediately, of course. He was too angry for that. But before he knew it, he was being ushered to the table where he'd seen Tranh and the others. Someone brought him something to drink.

And by the time he thought to look for Kane again, the man was gone.

Geordi was impressed. He'd only completed that spectrographic analysis the night before. The captain could hardly have had time to study it in depth, much less call his chief engineer to his ready room for a discussion of it.

But call he had. And when Captain Picard called, you didn't ask questions. You just did what you were told.

Before Geordi knew it, the turbolift doors were parting in front of him, revealing the ordered symmetry of the *Enterprise's* main bridge. Riker and Troi were in their customary places on either side of the command center, but the center seat was empty. Worf, who was manning the Tactical station as usual, gave him a quick glance as he emerged from the lift.

The Klingon's dark eyes inquired as to the reason for his presence here. At a loss, Geordi shrugged. No doubt, he would know more by the time he passed Worf on his way out.

"Geordi," he began, "one of the most important things in a man's life is the need to feel useful. Captain Scott is a Starfleet officer, even after all these years. I would like him to feel useful once again, if that is at all possible."

Ah. Finally, Geordi understood what the captain was saying. It was evident in the set of his jaw . . . in the cast of his eyes.

He was speaking not only for Scott, but for himself. For Geordi. For everyone who served on starships. One day, he was saying, the time would come when they too would be considered yesterday's news. And if they were to be treated with dignity *then*, they would have to set the best example they could in the here and now.

Geordi smiled reassuringly. "I'll go with him, Captain."

Picard nodded approvingly. "Thank you, Mr. La Forge. Unless there is anything else, you are dismissed."

"Thank you, sir," said Geordi. As he left the room, he was already figuring out the best way to tender his apology to Captain Scott.

Will Riker happened to be standing beside Worf at Tactical when Geordi emerged from the captain's ready room. The chief engineer looked as if he'd been kept after school, and for good reason.

Riker knew better than to ask what their conference had been about. If it was important for him to be told, Picard would have done so. And since he hadn't . . .

With a nod, Geordi crossed to the turbolift and entered it. The doors closed.

Worf's only response was something between a grunt and a snarl. But then, as the first officer was well aware, that sound covered a broad range of commentary.

"My thoughts exactly," Riker told him. And then, having satisfied himself that the Klingon's analyses were proceeding as they should be, he descended to the command center and deposited himself in his customary place.

"Commander Riker?" Mr. Data, who was stationed at Ops this shift, had turned in his seat to address him.

"Yes, Data?" The first officer leaned forward. "Something interesting?"

"I can only speak for myself," the android told him, "but *I* find it *very* interesting. I believe I have found something on the surface of the sphere that could be a communications device."

That got Riker out of his seat again. As he moved to Data's side, he began to scan the Ops console.

"There is a small antenna approximately five hundred thousand kilometers south of our present position," the android explained. "It is emitting low-intensity subspace signals that suggest it may be active."

"Can we open a channel?" asked the first officer.

Data shook his head. "Not from our present orbit, Commander. The array is currently pointed away from us."

Riker turned to Rager, who was manning the conn. "Have you got the coordinates of the array in question, Ensign?"

Rager worked at her control board for a second or two. "Aye, sir," she reported at last. "I've got them."

"Good," said the first officer. "Prepare to take us to a position above these coordinates."

As the ensign got to work again, Riker asked himself if this wouldn't be a good time to let the captain know what they were doing. He answered himself in the affirmative.

"Riker to Captain Picard," he intoned.

The reply was almost instantaneous. "Yes, Number One?"

"Sir, we've found what looks to be a communications array on the outside of the sphere. I thought you'd want to know."

A pause. "I'll be right out," the captain told him.

When Geordi got to the transporter room, there was nobody there but O'Brien. Crossing to the platform, the engineer plunked down the equipment case he'd been carrying and shrugged.

"Guess I'm early," he said.

O'Brien consulted his control board. "Only by thirty seconds or so," he judged. "That would make the rest of the away team—"

"Right on time," said Scott, as he walked in through the transporter room doors. His skin had a pale, almost greenish tinge to it, which made the bags under his eyes look even darker by contrast.

"Are you feeling all right?" Geordi asked him.

A little irritably, Scott responded: "Never get drunk unless ye're willing to pay for it the next day. I'll manage, thanks."

"Okay," said Geordi. Under the circumstances, he wasn't going to pry.

With only a small effort, the older man negotiated

the ascent to the platform. Turning to O'Brien, he nodded to signify his readiness.

Geordi picked up his equipment case and moved to stand beside Scott. "All right," he said. "Energize."

Picard regarded the main viewscreen, which showed a close shot of the surface of the sphere. There was a large, round outline on the metallic exterior with several small dish antennae around the perimeter of it.

"What is that circular shape?" he asked.

Data, who was seated in front of him at his Ops controls, turned to look up at him. "Sensor readings indicate that it is a hatch or airlock, sir—possibly one that leads into the interior of the sphere."

"I see," said the captain. He exchanged glances with Riker, who was standing next to him. "And you said you found a communications antenna?"

"Aye, sir," the android replied. "It is located on the periphery of the hatch at approximately seventeen degrees relative."

Picard took a breath and slowly let it out. "Fascinating," he remarked. "Absolutely fascinating."

"This looks like the front door," Riker noted. "Should we ring the bell?"

The captain thought about it for a moment—and came to a decision. "Let's do just that, Number One. Mister Worf, try to open a channel to that comm antenna."

"Aye, sir," said the Klingon, setting to work at his Tactical console. After a few seconds, he reported: "Nothing yet."

"Keep at it," said Riker. "It may take a—"

"Captain!" cried Rager. She looked up from her conn board, her face a mask of alarm. "Intense graviton emissions on the surface of the sphere! And they're heading this—!"

Before the ensign could finish her warning, the ship was rocked—and rocked hard. Picard was flung across the deck like a rag doll, finally coming up against the base of a bulkhead with spine-jarring impact. For a moment, he flirted with unconsciousness. Then, with an almost physical effort, he pulled himself up out of it.

What he saw was a twilight version of his bridge. Illumination was down. Several consoles had gone out. And his officers, with the exception of Data, had been strewn from one end of the place to the other. Like him, they were dazed . . . just starting to pick themselves up.

"Red alert," he called out, managing to be heard over the increasing murmurs of pain and surprise. Then he staggered over to Moreno, who had fallen facedown near one of the aft stations and still wasn't moving.

Feeling her neck for her pulse, he found it—but it was slower than it should have been. And there was a deep, bloody gash in her forehead near the hairline—one that needed tending, and quickly.

"Dr. Crusher," he barked, hoping that the intercom system hadn't been damaged.

The doctor's response was nearly immediate. "I know," she said. "You've got casualties on the bridge. We've got them all over the ship." A pause. "I'm sending up a trauma team. Crusher out."

"Captain Picard?" It was Data, still sitting at his

station as if he'd been nailed down. "We have been caught in some type of tractor beam, sir. It is drawing us down to the sphere's outer surface."

The android said it so matter-of-factly, his voice so devoid of emotion, that the danger almost didn't seem real. But it was real, all right. As real as the blood running down the side of Moreno's face.

By then, Riker had pulled himself back into his seat in the command center. "Helm!" he cried. "Get us out of here! Impulse engines, back full!"

"We've lost main power," reported Rager. She too had been injured; her cheek was badly lacerated. "Auxiliary power down to twenty percent!"

Picard felt his teeth grinding together as he considered the irony: They'd come to rescue the *Jenolen,* but now they themselves needed rescue.

Would they survive the crash, as Scott had survived? Or would the *Enterprise*'s greater mass seal their collective doom?

"Run the impulse engines off auxiliary," Riker commanded. "If we can't back off, let's at least try to slow down!"

But it was too late for that; the captain could feel it in his bones. As they approached the surface of the Dyson Sphere, their rate of descent was actually increasing. Even at full power, they'd have their hands full avoiding disaster. The sphere was looming closer and closer, larger and larger . . .

And then, as if by divine decree, the skin of the sphere started to part . . . started to crack open just a hair. The hairline crack became a fissure. The fissure became a chasm, the chasm a veritable canyon.

"It's a hatch," muttered Riker.

"Indeed," Picard confirmed.

Suddenly, a blaze of light shot out at them, blinding them with its yellow-white brilliance—a brilliance that could not have contrasted more vividly with the sphere's dark surface. Shielding his eyes, the captain thought he knew what it was.

A moment later, the viewscreen's light filter automatically clamped down a notch, and they could see where the explosion of light had originated. Picard had been right.

It was the star at the center of the construct. The star that the makers of the sphere had captured and shut off from the rest of the universe—like some colossal slave, like a leviathan of burden. Like Prometheus, the fire-bringer of the myths . . . bound for all eternity.

Worf glared at the screen, his eyes wild with apprehension and fury. "The beam is too strong. We can't resist it!"

"It is not just *one* tractor beam," observed Data, the perfect counterpoint to the Klingon's intensity. "There are *six* of them, sir."

The captain could see them now: a half-dozen faint tentacles of light, emanating at intervals from the somber and featureless lip of the hatch, inexorably drawing the *Enterprise* to its fate.

"We're being pulled inside!" Worf roared.

And so they were. They were hurtling toward the mighty hatch, falling into a hole that was gaping wider and wider to consume them—drawn inexorably to their fate.

And there was nothing they could do about it. *Nothing.*

Chapter Ten

RIKER IGNORED the taste of blood in his mouth and tried to get a handle on what was happening to the *Enterprise*. It wasn't easy.

Seconds ago, the hatch in the Dyson Sphere had closed behind them, trapping them within. And in that same moment, the stars had disappeared, replaced with a bluish-green sky.

But they still weren't slowing down. He could tell by the readouts on the monitor that projected from his armrest. They were still plunging headlong toward the center of the sphere—and at the center was the hideous, glorious *sun*.

The impulse engines were struggling mightily against the forces that had pulled them in. The ship trembled with the effort, lights flickering on the bridge as engineering greedily sucked up what little power they had left. But it was all to no avail.

Only moments ago, the first officer had been glad to see the hatch opening in the sphere. It had meant they weren't going to splatter themselves all over the thing's surface.

Now he felt a little differently. At least a collision would have yielded them some hope of survival. Hell, the *Jenolen* had crashed and stayed largely intact, hadn't it? But plunging into the heart of a star, captive or otherwise, was a death sentence no one escaped from.

"Auxiliary power failing," said Rager. There were beads of sweat forming on her forehead; she wiped at them with her sleeve.

"Hull temperature approaching maximum tolerance levels," announced Worf. His lips were drawn back over his teeth in an expression of defiance.

"We are passing through the sphere's interior atmosphere," said Data. "The resulting friction on the hull is causing the increase."

"Raise shields," commanded Riker, dreading the response.

"Minimal shield power," snarled Worf. "Hull temperature now *critical.*"

Data turned to look at the captain, who was still kneeling beside Moreno, the fallen crew member. "The resonance frequency of the tractor beams is incompatible with our power systems. Warp and impulse engine relays have been overloaded. I am attempting to compensate."

Moreno chose that moment to moan softly and roll over. She tried to get up, but Picard restrained her.

"You've suffered a wound to the head," he told her.

155

"Lie still until we can get Dr. Crusher to examine you."

The woman looked up at him. "Aye, sir," she said dutifully, wincing at the pain her wound was causing her.

The captain turned to Data again. "How long, Commander?"

"Difficult to say, sir," the android replied. His fingers were flying over his control panel as fast as the computer could respond. "It depends on how extensively the circuits have been damaged."

The captain frowned and looked to his first officer. Riker frowned back. They both knew that Data's efforts would prove futile. Even if he got the connections rerouted, they didn't have the engine power to fight the sphere's tractor beams.

Riker felt a drop of sweat roll down the side of his face. Damn, he thought. It *was* getting hot in here, wasn't it? Though it was nothing compared to the temperatures in that furnace of a sun dead ahead.

At the sound of the turbolift doors opening, he turned and saw Beverly Crusher emerge with a couple of nurses and a stretcher. Dropping down to her knees beside Moreno in one fluid motion, the doctor ran her tricorder over the woman's head and neck area.

"Minor concussion," she concluded. "Can you walk?" she asked Moreno.

"I . . . I think so," her patient said. And to demonstrate, she got to her feet, albeit with Picard's help. Then, turning to the captain, she asked: "Sir . . . if it's all right with you, can I stay on the bridge to help?"

The captain's voice was firm. "I'll find it more

helpful knowing that you're receiving the attention you need."

"I agree," said Crusher. "Come on." And putting her arm around Moreno, she ushered her in the direction of the lift.

But before she actually got in, the doctor took a look at the viewscreen, and the ball of fire with which they were due to collide. Then she caught sight of Riker and saw the hard cast of his eyes.

"Good luck," she told him. A moment later, she and her people had entered the lift and the doors were whispering shut behind them.

There had to be something they could do, the first officer told himself. Hadn't they been in impossible positions before? And hadn't they always managed to somehow get out of them? If only . . .

Before he could complete the thought, the *Enterprise* shuddered violently and wrenched them out of their seats again. This time, Riker was better prepared; he was able to grab his monitor, or he would have been flipped halfway across the deck a second time.

The shaking stopped as abruptly as it had begun. The first officer got to his feet and looked around. No one seemed badly injured, though as before, only Data had kept his seat. He turned to the viewscreen, hoping he'd get some clue as to what had happened.

He wasn't disappointed. The bluish sky on the main viewer had faded away and was replaced by a clearer view of the captive star. The interior surface of the sphere could be dimly seen in the far distance.

"We've cleared the atmosphere," reported Lieutenant Worf. "Hull temperature dropping back to safety levels."

"But we're still headed for the sun," the captain reminded them. Pulling down on the front of his tunic, he descended to the command center and came to stand beside Riker. "Suggestions?"

"What the . . .?" The exclamation came from Rager.

The first officer looked at her. "Something, Ensign?"

Rager shook her head in disbelief. "The tractor beams have released us, sir." She broke out into a grin. "We're free."

Was it possible? Riker checked it out on his monitor. Sure enough, there was no longer any evidence of the sphere's tractor beams. He grunted. A stroke of luck—not that he was complaining.

"Hold position here," he told Rager. "At least until we can get our bearings." They needed time to lick their wounds, to regroup. To figure out what in blazes to do next.

Picard turned to his second officer. "Full sensor sweep, Mr. Data. Where are we?"

"We are approximately ninety million kilometers from the star's photosphere," came the answer. Data paused, making adjustments in his sensor controls. "Sensors record—"

Suddenly, Rager broke in. "Sir . . . the inertial motion from the tractor beams is still carrying us forward."

Riker exchanged glances with the captain as he descended to the conn. Rager was shaking her head.

"The impulse engines are off-line," she said, "and the maneuvering system's been shorted out." She looked up at Riker helplessly. "I can't stop our forward momentum, sir."

Figures, the first officer thought. I should have known it was too good to be true. I should have *smelled* it.

"The inertial motion imparted by the tractor beams is carrying us directly toward the star," Data added— as calmly as if he were reciting poetry.

But those who heard his pronouncement weren't nearly so calm about it. Suddenly, they were back on the firing line.

"Come on," said Scott—rather gently, Geordi thought. Maybe too gently. "Ye can do it. I know ye can."

He was talking to an open computer panel in the Ops center of the *Jenolen,* trying to coax the system into working. La Forge scanned the readout on the diagnostic device he'd brought in his equipment case. Hooked up to the console above the opening, it was blinking and flashing in response to Scott's machinations.

"Dinnae give me a hard time now," the older man scolded. "Or I'll just let ye sit there and gather dust for *another* seventy-five years."

But despite the banter, Scott didn't seem to have his heart in it. There was something missing . . . the fire that had made him such a pain in the neck back in engineering, the brazen self-confidence that had eventually caused Geordi to blow up at him.

It didn't take an empath to see that he'd been demoralized. And though it wasn't all his fault, the younger man had certainly had a hand in that.

La Forge had meant to apologize to Scott as soon as they boarded the *Jenolen*. He really had. But there was something in the man's demeanor that said he wouldn't want to hear it . . . that it actually might have made him feel worse.

So Geordi had refrained from mentioning the incident in the engine room. But that didn't mean he wasn't going to try to make amends. He would just bide his time and look for the proper opening.

"Ah," said Scott. He nodded approvingly. "There we go." He turned to his companion. "The primary computer database should be on-line now. Give 'er a try, Commander."

Geordi made some adjustments and took another look at his readout. A couple of lights flashed on the face of the device.

"Okay," he said. "I've got three access lines to the central core now." He frowned, wishing he had better news. "But still no data."

Scott cursed beneath his breath. "I thought I had it that time." Thinking for a moment, he applied himself to the open panel again. "Here, maybe this'll do it. Hell, it'd better." After a minute of remanipulating the circuitry, he sat back on his haunches. "Let 'er rip."

Geordi did as he was instructed. There was no improvement.

"Nothing?" said the older man.

"Nothing *yet,*" La Forge corrected. But the distinction seemed to have been lost on Scott. He shook his head, too irritated to continue.

Softly, he said: "Bunch of old, useless garbage . . ."

"What?" asked Geordi.

Scott sighed. "I said it's old, Mr. La Forge. The controller can't handle the interface of your new power converter."

Scott opened another panel and began tinkering with the inner workings. After a moment, however, he gave up.

"This equipment was designed for a different era," Scott went on. "Now it's just a lot of junk." The older man looked depressed.

He was talking about more than just the equipment, Geordi realized. He was talking about himself.

"I don't know," said Geordi. "Looks to me like some of it has held together pretty well."

Scott looked at him disbelievingly. "Come on," he said. "Ye cannae mean that, lad. It's a century out of date. How can ye use something that antiquated? It's just . . ." He slammed the panel closed in disgust. "Obsolete," he finished.

Geordi wanted to reach out to the man in some way. He considered the console he was working on and ran his hand over it.

"That's interesting, Mr. Scott . . . because I was just thinking that a lot of these systems haven't changed much in seventy-five years."

Scott was barely paying attention. He was too wrapped up in his own thoughts. Geordi moved over to the transporter console.

"Aside from a few minor improvements," he went

on, "this transporter is virtually identical to the ones we use on the *Enterprise*." He gestured to the other consoles. "The subspace radio and sensors operate on the same basic principles, and impulse engine design hasn't changed much in almost two hundred years. If it weren't for the structural damage, this ship could still be in service today."

Scott considered what Geordi was saying. "Maybe so," he replied. "But when ye can build a ship like her *Enterprise*, a twenty-fourth century marvel of technology . . . who'd want to pilot an old bucket like this one?"

"I don't know," said Geordi appraisingly. "The *Enterprise* has her strengths, but she's also got her weaknesses. Fix that engine and I bet this ship would run circles around her at impulse speeds." A beat. "Just because something's old doesn't mean you have to throw it away."

They looked at each other for a moment. Geordi could feel something happening between them. A bond was forming. Maybe even a friendship. Scott was the one who finally dissolved the moment, moving back to the computer console.

"We used to have something called a dynamic mode converter," he mused out loud. Ye would nae have something like that in yer fancy new *Enterprise*, would ye?"

Geordi thought about it for a second or two. "I haven't seen one of those in a long time. But I might have something similar."

Hitting his communicator emblem, he said: "La Forge to *Enterprise*."

No one answered. Geordi hit the emblem again.

"La Forge to *Enterprise,* come in please."

Still nothing. How strange . . .

Scott darted him a look of concern. Geordi moved to the sensor console.

"Interference?" asked Scott.

Geordi worked the sensor controls. "No. Unfortunately."

A moment later, the sensor monitors showed him the astounding truth. "Damn," he whispered.

"What is it?" Scott pressed.

Geordi turned to him. "They're *gone.* "

"We will enter the sun's photosphere in three minutes," said Data.

"Helm control still inoperative," Rager reported.

Picard tried his best to stay calm, to keep a clear head. But it was easier said than done. The captive star filled the main viewscreen as the *Enterprise* rushed toward it—as if eager to feel its nuclear-fusion embrace.

There had to be a way out of this. He wouldn't accept defeat—not while he had a brain and some time to use it.

Suddenly, it came to him. He turned to Riker, who had replaced Moreno at the aft engineering station— where Geordi would have been if he hadn't beamed over to the *Jenolen.*

"Number One—are the maneuvering thrusters on-line?" he asked.

Though his expression said he failed to see what the captain was getting at, Riker worked furiously at the controls. After a second or two, he nodded.

"I've got thirty percent power on the starboard

thrusters. Fifteen percent on the port thrusters. But it won't be enough to brake our inertia."

"No," agreed Picard. "But it may just be enough to put us in orbit and hold our distance from the star."

For a brief moment, Riker smiled. Then he turned to the monitor again, preparing himself for what was ahead.

Next, the captain addressed his android second officer. "Mr. Data—calculate the minimum change in our trajectory necessary to avoid the star."

It seemed that Data's answer began before Picard's question was finished. "A twenty-degree turn will allow the ship to enter a safe orbit around the star."

The captain whirled toward the engineering station. "Did you hear that, Number One?"

"I did, sir," came the reply. "Twenty degrees . . ."

There was a silent "if" hanging on the end of that phrase. As in *if I can do it*. Even a twenty-degree variation would be a prodigious task under these conditions. And if they managed only nineteen degrees? There would be nothing left of them but cinders.

"Port thrusters ahead full, starboard back full."

"Aye, sir," called the first officer, following Picard's orders.

As Riker bent to his task, the captain glanced at the viewscreen. The star was terribly close; he could almost feel its fury on his face. If his plan didn't work, they were goners. It was as simple as that.

"Our flight path is changing," Data announced.

"Right ten point seven degrees . . . insufficient to clear the photosphere."

Riker looked up at the intercom grid. "Bridge to engineering. Lieutenant Bartel—divert all power from auxiliary relay systems to the maneuvering thrusters."

"Our angular deflection is increasing," observed the android. "Now at fifteen degrees . . . eighteen degrees . . . turn now at twenty point one degrees."

Picard looked at the viewscreen. Would it be enough? Could Data have miscalculated? The sun at the center of the sphere was looming larger and larger . . .

And then, as the captain held his breath, the giant viewscreen image of the star finally shifted to the left . . . then more . . . and still more . . . as the ship managed to turn away from it. Finally, they passed the outer edges of the photosphere to starboard—if only *just.*

There was a collective sigh of relief, almost as if the bridge itself were exhaling. Picard realized his hands had become fists; he relaxed them.

In front of him, Rager's shoulders unclenched. "We're in orbit, Captain. Holding at one hundred fifty thousand kilometers above the photosphere."

"I'll see about getting main power back on-line," Riker volunteered.

"Very well," said Picard. As Riker exited the bridge, he took his seat and leaned back into it. That had been, as they say, a close one. "Mr. Data, begin a scan of the interior surface for life-forms. I want to know who brought us here . . . and why."

"Aye, sir," said Data, already complying with the captain's command.

The captain wished he could get word to the *Jenolen* somehow. But Geordi and Scott would be all right— at least for the time being.

Chapter Eleven

IT HAD BEEN a long time since anyone had attempted to use the sensor controls in the Ops center of the transport vessel *Jenolen*. All things considered, they were in remarkably good shape.

Working alongside Scott, Geordi pushed the ship's scanners to their limits. But try as he might, he couldn't turn up so much as a blip.

"I can't find them anywhere in orbit," he said out loud.

"No luck here either," replied his companion.

"They wouldn't have just upped and left," Geordi insisted.

"Nae even fer an emergency?" asked Scott.

The younger man shook his head. "They would've beamed us back aboard first. Or at least let us know what they were going."

Scott nodded his head. "Aye. I guess they would've at that." Suddenly, his brow furrowed. "Ye dinnae suppose they crashed into the sphere . . . just as the *Jenolen* did?"

Geordi rejected the idea. "No. We'd be picking up background radiation and debris if they'd gone down like that." He bit his lip. "But then, where are they? They couldn't have just vanished into the void."

For a moment, neither of them spoke. Then Scott's eyes narrowed with thought. "There's another possibility," he ventured. "They could be *inside* the sphere."

Geordi looked at him. At first blush, it sounded preposterous. Ridiculous. But the more he considered it . . . "Maybe," he said. "Yeah. Maybe."

"Nae just *maybe*," his companion countered. "They're in there. It's the only place they could be, lad."

The younger man took a breath and let it out. "Whatever's happened, we've got to find them. If we can get these engines back on-line, we could track the *Enterprise* by its impulse ion trail."

Suddenly, Scott turned livid. He held out his hands palms-up to show his helplessness. "Are ye daft?" he asked. "The main drive assembly's completely shot, the inducers are melted and the power couplings are wrecked. We'd need a week just to get *started!*"

Geordi felt the anger building inside him, crawling up his throat—ready to burst forth from his mouth. First he couldn't get this guy to stand aside—and now he couldn't convince him to help. No matter what he promised the captain, he'd taken about all he could—

"Wait a minute," said Scott. He stroked his chin for a second or two . . . and then went on like the most reasonable man you'd ever want to meet. "We dinnae have a week, now do we? So there's no sense cryin' about it. Come on. Let's see what we can do with that power converter ye're so fond of."

Then, turning away from Geordi, Scott made his way toward the engines—leaving the younger man a little surprised. With a bemused look, he followed his predecessor's lead.

As tenuous as their situation was as they orbited the captive sun, Picard could not help but remember his mission. As he'd told Data not too long before, they had gone out into space to seek out new life and new civilizations—and the builders of this Dyson Sphere promised to represent the strangest civilization of all.

It was at least part of the reason he had asked his second officer to examine the inside of the solar system–sized construct. The other part was based on a more selfish motivation: survival.

Someone had gone to the trouble of drawing them inside this thing. It was incumbent on them to find this someone if they were to have any serious hope of reopening the hatch and gaining their freedom.

Unfortunately, Lieutenant Worf had already analyzed the sphere's composition and discovered it to be composed of carbon-neutronium—one of the hardest substances known to the Federation. Even at full power, they could not generate a phaser barrage strong enough to punch a hole in the outer shell.

"Captain?"

Picard traced the call to its source: one of the aft science stations. "Yes, Data. Have you got something already?"

"I do, sir."

It was difficult to tell from the android's expression, which was as deadpan as ever, just what it was he had. Containing his curiosity for just another moment, the captain joined his second officer.

"I have completed the bio scan of the interior surface of the sphere," Data informed him.

Picard took a look at the monitor, where the evidence was plain to see. His hopes sank. "No life," he concluded.

The android looked almost sympathetic. "That is correct, sir. The sphere appears to be abandoned. Although . . ." He switched to another graphic—one that mapped out the surface of the sphere in terms of sensor efficiency. ". . . our instruments seem incapable of probing a small area . . . right *there.*"

Picard followed Data's finger as he pointed to the spot in question. The captain grunted. "In other words," he said, "we do not know if there is any life in that location or not."

"We do not," the android confirmed. "Of course, one might conclude that since the rest of the surface has apparently been deserted—"

"That this section has been deserted as well," the captain remarked, completing his second officer's thought. "On the other hand, if this area is shielded from our sensors, it may have been shielded for a reason." He reflected on the possibility. "Say, by a group who elected to stay in the sphere when the others left—and wished to remain hidden from any who might enter here."

"True, sir," said Data. "Nor will we know for certain one way or the other—unless we send an away team down to investigate."

Picard turned to him. "Are you advocating that, Data?"

"I am merely stating a fact," said the android.

The captain mulled over the advisability of sending down an away team. Power reserves were still low. With various systems down, the ship was not as maneuverable as he would have liked.

However, the sensor-shielded area would be below them in less than an hour. This might be their only chance—not only to make contact with an obviously superior race, but to rescue themselves from the sphere. Could he pass it up just like that?

Finally, he looked up. "Commander Riker, this is the captain."

A moment later, the first officer responded. "We've still got some work ahead of us, sir. Some of the relays were blown and it'll take time to replace them."

"Understood, Number One. But that is not why I contacted you." He paused. "I would like you to gather an away team."

There was silence on the other end. Finally, Riker said: "An away team, sir?"

"Yes." Picard turned to Data's monitor. "I need you to do some exploring, Will. And I need you to do it quickly."

Darrin Kane was in Shuttlebay One, a place he was starting to hate as much as the cargo holds, when he heard his name being called over the intercom system —and by his favorite person, Will Riker.

What numbing torture had the first officer devised for him now? Was he to report to the Ten-Forward lounge and wait tables?

"Kane here," he said, resisting a whispered curse. With his luck, the intercom would probably be sensitive enough to pick it up.

"Report to Shuttlebay Three," said Riker. "I'm putting together an away team and you're on it."

The ensign could scarcely believe his ears. "An away team?" he repeated. Was this some kind of joke? Was he going to arrive at the shuttlebay only to find that the mission had been cancelled—or that Riker had left without him?

"Mr. Kane? Don't tell me you're sleeping up *there* now."

"Uh . . . no, sir," replied Kane.

"Five minutes," the first officer told him. "Don't be late."

"No, Commander. I mean *yes,* Commander. I mean . . ." Abruptly, he realized he was talking to the shuttlecraft. Riker had broken the connection.

Kane shook his head and sought out Lieutenant Bridges, who was in charge of the shuttlebay for this shift. Bridges was running a routine check on the bay doors when he finally found her.

"Something wrong?" she asked.

"I'm not sure," Kane told her. "Commander Riker wants me to be on an away team."

She looked at him askance. "An away team? Away *where?*"

The ensign was about to provide an answer . . .

until he realized he didn't have one. "I don't know," he told her. "But I've got to get going."

And leaving her standing there, he took off for Shuttlebay Three.

Sousa stood in the Shuttlebay between Commander Riker and Counselor Troi. Bartel and Krause from engineering were there as well. Now the only one they were still missing was Darrin Kane.

A moment later, the doors to the corridor whooshed open and Kane came trotting in. He was all business, no doubt glad for such a juicy assignment after all the low-key jobs to which he'd been relegated.

As he joined the group, he took in the rest of the away team with a glance—and then did a double-take when he saw his fellow ensign standing in their midst. Sousa smiled by way of a greeting, trying to let Kane know there were no hard feelings.

But he got no response. Kane just took his spot and faced Riker. It was as if he and Sousa had never been friends at all.

"Ready, sir," said Kane.

The first officer nodded, scanning each face in turn. "Here's the way it's going to work. Normally, we would just beam down. But the ship is in no condition to leave orbit—and since the surface is so far away, the only way for us to get there is by shuttle." He paused. "Unfortunately, our scanners show us that there's no place near our destination that's big enough to accommodate a shuttle. So we're going to hover a couple of hundred meters from the landing site and beam down two at a time using the emergency transporter. Any questions?"

Sousa had one. "How are we going to get back?"

"A remote control link will allow us to return via the transporter," said Riker. "We'll also have the option of bringing the shuttle down if we find something too big to beam up."

Sousa nodded. "Understood, sir."

"All right, then, said the first officer. "Let's board."

In the Ops center of the *Jenolen,* Geordi was lying on his back with only his legs sticking out from beneath a control console. Less than a meter away, Scott was in the same position under a neighboring console. Various tools and diagnostic devices were scattered around the deck, waiting to be used or reused.

It had been hours since Geordi had agreed to help get the *Jenolen's* engines started. But in that time, he and Scott had made more progress than he would have imagined possible. Every power conduit and relay circuit was back on line. If the engines themselves hadn't been damaged beyond repair, they actually stood a chance of getting this vessel moving again.

The man may not have a perfect grasp of modern technology, La Forge told himself. But when it comes to engineering principles and the twenty-third century, he really knows his stuff. In fact, I'd be surprised if anyone of his time knew it better.

"Shunt the deuterium from the main cryo pump to the auxiliary tank," Scott recommended.

"The tank won't hold up under that much pressure," Geordi told him, poking his head out for a moment.

The older man poked his head out as well. "Where'd ye get that idea, laddie?"

Geordi shrugged. "It's in the impulse engine specifications."

"Regulation forty-two slash fifteen alpha? 'Pressure Variances in IRC Tank Storage?'"

"Right."

"Forget it," said Scott. "I wrote the bloody thing."

Withdrawing his head below the console again, he continued his commentary as he worked. "A good engineer is always a wee bit conservative, Commander." He chuckled. "At least on paper. Just bypass the secondary cut-off valve and boost the flow. It'll work —trust me."

Smiling to himself, Geordi hauled himself to his feet and made the necessary adjustments on the console's control panel. "Okay," he said. "I'm shunting the deuterium."

This had better work, he mused, or we'll both be little puffs of free-floating gases.

A moment passed. Two. If there was going to be a problem in the auxiliary tank, it probably would've manifested itself by now.

"Well?" asked the older man.

"So far so good," Geordi reported. "Looks like you were right."

Scott grunted. "Naturally, lad." Crawling out from under his own console, he cracked his knuckles and, with a bit of a flourish, pressed a few buttons.

"What are you doing?" asked Geordi. "We're not at the moment of truth yet . . . are we?"

It seemed to him there were still a couple of tests to

be made first. But then, Scott's methods were a little different from his.

"Well," said the older man, "let me put it this way. If we've done our jobs properly, the engines should be coming back on-line about . . . *now.*"

For a moment, they watched the display and nothing happened. Then, slowly, console by dead console, the remainder of the Ops center came to life. The place was rife with blinking lights.

Geordi laughed, as delighted as a child who'd just been taught a new trick. He checked his levels. "And the auxiliary tank is still holding."

Scott flashed a grin at him and then indicated the *Jenolen*'s small command chair. "The bridge is yours, Commander."

Geordi held up a hand to demur. "Uh, uh. You're the senior officer here."

"I may be a captain by rank," Scott conceded, "but I've never *wanted* to be anything but an *engineer.* Take the conn, Geordi."

For a moment, Geordi found himself admiring the hell out of Captain Montgomery Scott. "All right," he said finally. "I'll take the conn."

Moving to the command chair, he sat down in it, while Scott made his way to the engineering panel. "Okay then," he said, examining the readouts in his armrest monitor. "Let's get going. We've got a starship to track down."

"Aye, sir," said the older man.

"Full impulse," said Geordi.

"Full impulse," Scott echoed.

And they were off.

* * *

"Energize."

Funny thing about transporters, thought Riker. The first time he'd used one, he'd expected there to be some sort of transitional feeling . . . some sensation of being gradually drawn out of one place and phased into another.

But it wasn't like that at all. One moment you were in the transporter room, the next you were standing on a planet or in a space station or on another ship. There was nothing in between, no period of adjustment. You were just, all of a sudden, *there*.

It was that way this time, too. Except this time, *there* was unlike anywhere else Riker had ever seen. Without meaning to, he said as much.

"If it's any consolation," Troi commented, "it's not like anything *I've* ever seen either."

Sousa looked around—first at the perfectly round plate on which they stood, which had been selected as the optimum landing sight. Then at the immense towers that jutted up into the green-blue sky all around them, stretching in an unbroken field to the strangely curving horizon. Ramps of various widths ran from tower to tower, all at the same level as their plate, and tremendous chasms yawned in the intervals between the towers.

Everything was a dark shade of purple. Everything was artificial. There were no breezes, no clouds, no plants, no vegetation . . . not even any dirt. And, in this spot at least, no evidence of sentient life.

But then, they hadn't exactly expected a welcome wagon. Their beam-down site was part of the area they'd already bio-scanned without success. It was the area their sensors *couldn't* probe—perhaps two hundred meters away—which still held the possibility of living sphere builders.

"Come on," said Riker, taking one last look at the shuttlecraft. Gesturing with his tricorder, he indicated the direction in which they had to travel. "Let's go. And be careful. Watch your footing."

Fortunately, a number of the ramps gave them the access they wanted. That was the good news. The bad news was that the ramps were narrow and zigzagging in that quarter—as if someone had wanted to make it difficult for anyone to go that way.

But that was ridiculous, Sousa told himself—wasn't it? Not everybody would be starting out from this plate, right? And if the builders had wanted to prevent anyone from going there, why have ramps at all?

Slowly, carefully, they set out across one of the chasms—one of the narrower ones. Sousa had no particular fear of heights, but still he tried not to look down. He didn't have to do any peering over the side to know it was a long way to the bottom.

As he walked, the ensign marveled at the ghostly quiet. Even their footfalls seemed to be absorbed into it—and swallowed, like pebbles in a great, dark pool.

Finally, they reached one of the towers. It had a number of arched entrances, one for each ramp that led to it—but no doors. Sousa tried to peer inside, but it was murky in there, shaded as it was from the sun—and the contrast was just too great for him to see anything.

Riker was the first one to enter the place, with Troi close behind and the rest of them bringing up the rear.

Even after they'd gotten out of the sunlight, it took a while for the ensign's eyes to adjust.

The first thing he noticed was a bank of what looked like monstrous machines lining one of the building's interior walls. Then, as he scanned the other walls, he saw the same thing. Machines that climbed high into the tower, so high they were lost in darkness and distance.

There were no floors above this level, Sousa observed. No stairwells and no elevators. Just empty space—and of course, the machines that shaped it with their presence.

"How do you suppose they got up there?" asked Krause, his voice echoing.

"The machines?" asked Sousa, his echoes answering the first set.

Krause shot him a look. "I mean the *builders*. There isn't even anything to stand on."

"Beats hell out of me," said Bartel. "Unless . . . they flew."

Sousa looked at *her*. "Flew?" he repeated. "You mean, like with wings?"

Bartel shrugged. "With or without. Maybe they just willed themselves up there—what's the difference? The point is, they got there on their own."

And a good point it was, he conceded. But there was no one here now, winged or otherwise. Since the machines were dead as well, there wasn't much to linger over. Once they'd recorded what they could with their tricorders, they moved on.

Once again, they had to make their way over the zigzagging ramps—longer ones this time. Because there wasn't enough room for more than two to walk abreast, the away team automatically strung itself out into three pairs. And they walked at intervals, to minimize the possibility of an unforeseen problem afflicting all of them at once. As luck would have it, Kane wound up walking beside Sousa.

Turning to him, Sousa said in a low voice: "A little spooky, isn't it?"

The other man glanced at him, but didn't respond. Instead, he made a show of using his tricorder to scan the stuff they were walking on.

"Come on," Sousa whispered. "Let's forget what we said, all right?"

But Kane wasn't buying it. His only response was a withering glance.

Sousa sighed. *Be that way,* he thought. *No skin off my nose.*

But when he looked around at the silent towers and the abysses that yawned below them, he wished he at least had someone to talk to. It would have made the going just a little more tolerable.

Chapter Twelve

JEAN-LUC PICARD knew his senior officers like the back of his hand. When there was something worrying one of them, he was aware of it, even if he couldn't always divine the details. And Commander Data, despite his lack of human emotions, was no exception.

So when the captain saw Data focusing more intently than usual at his Ops controls, his artificial brow creased ever so slightly with concentration, he went to the android's side immediately. For Data, that was the equivalent of a panicked scream.

"What is it?" asked Picard.

Data looked up at him. "A problem, sir."

Working his controls, he brought up a schematic diagram of the sphere and its captive sun. Several sections of the star were highlighted and magnified.

"Our sensors show that this star is extremely

unstable," the android explained. "It is prone to severe bursts of radiation and matter expulsions."

The captain scowled. "That would explain why the sphere is abandoned." He looked to the main viewscreen, with the image of the captive sun emblazoned on it. "Is the away team in danger?" he asked his second officer.

"I do not believe so," said Data. "While solar radiation has made the sphere uninhabitable over the long term, it should not present a hazard in the short term." He paused. "At least not to the away team."

Picard regarded his second officer. "To us, then?"

Data nodded. "The away team is much farther away from the sun than we are. At our current distance, with our shields virtually inoperative, a solar flare would pose a significant danger to the crew."

The captain nodded, taking the android's advice to heart. "All the more reason to get our shields up to full power again—as soon as possible."

Data nodded, expressionless—except for that slight crease in his forehead. "That would be wise, sir."

Riker tapped his communicator one last time and waited. Finally, he shook his head. "Nothing," he said. "Nada. Zip."

Troi nodded. "Whatever is thwarting our sensor probe is also preventing communications with the ship. Hardly unexpected," she said.

"Hardly," he agreed. "Still, it would have been nice to find out we were wrong—at least in this regard. I don't like the idea of being cut off from the bridge." He looked around. "Especially in a jungle gym like this one."

The counselor smiled. "We will be fine."

"Is that just encouragement?" he asked. "Or are you getting into the predictions game now?"

She shrugged. "We Betazoids have all kinds of talents."

Riker grunted, "You're telling me."

Troi gave Riker a withering stare, but soon couldn't resist a grin.

It felt good to crack a joke or two, Riker thought. So far, their mission had been an uneventful and frustrating one. As many ramps as they negotiated, the result was always the same. Every tower was as empty as the first one they'd explored: lots of big machines that weren't giving up any secrets.

No clues as to what had happened to the builders. Nothing to really indicate what their race might have been like. And no evidence that any of them were still alive.

A few minutes ago, they had reached a large, round plate just inside the sensor-shielded section—not unlike the structure onto which they'd beamed down. Riker had called for a break while he tried to contact the ship.

But now, break time was over. "All right," he told the rest of his team. He pointed to the cluster of towers up ahead. "Let's stay together. And keep our eyes open."

Picard was still standing beside Data, watching the image of the captive star on the main viewscreen. He shook his head.

"Automatic piloting beams, eh?"

The android nodded. "Yes. I believe they were designed to guide ships inside the sphere."

"And our communications attempt triggered them?"

"Precisely, sir. Then the resonant frequency of the beams interfered with the integrity of our main power system, temporarily taking the engines off-line."

The captain took a deep breath, then let it out. "All right. That makes sense. Would you care to hazard a guess as to how we can use this information to get ourselves out again?"

Data didn't look hopeful. "Unfortunately, that is a different matter en—"

Suddenly, Worf broke into their conversation. His voice carried a sense of terrible urgency—and Klingons didn't show that kind of concern easily.

"Sir, sensors show a large magnetic disturbance on the star's surface."

"A magnetic disturbance?" Picard echoed.

Data worked the controls on his console at a speed only he could manage. "It is a solar flare, Captain. Magnitude: twelve. Class: B."

Picard turned back to Worf. "Shields, Lieutenant?"

The Klingon scowled. "Shields up . . . but only at twenty-three percent."

"Magnify," the captain commanded. He wanted to see what they were up against.

Abruptly, the screen showed a huge solar flare reaching out from the star. It was heading directly toward the *Enterprise*.

Picard felt the muscles in his face drawing tight. At this range, twenty-three percent might not be equal to the task.

"The star has entered a period of increased activity."

"Just like that?" asked the captain.

Data nodded. "Apparently, sir. And our sensor readings indicate that the solar flare trend will continue to grow. In three hours, our shields will not be sufficient to protect us."

"Damn," whispered someone at one of the aft stations.

My sentiments exactly, thought Picard.

They were deep into the shielded area now. And still nothing to write home about, Riker thought. The towers they'd investigated here were much like those they'd seen earlier. Hell, as far as he could tell, they were *exactly* like those they'd seen earlier.

He turned to Troi, who was still walking beside him. As before, she was focusing her empathic powers on their next destination. The first officer watched her face for some sign of discovery. There wasn't any.

"We're on a wild-goose chase," he said softly. "Aren't we?"

"It is a little too soon to say," she replied.

"No, it's not. Not for you," he pressed. "If there were somebody here, you would have known it already. You would have sensed them."

The counselor bit her lip. "There are minds to which I cannot gain access," she reminded him. "The builders of this place may fall into that category. They may be so different from us—so emotionless, perhaps —that they simply do not register with me."

"But more likely," he suggested, "they're just not around anymore." He indicated the towers ahead of them with a sweep of his arm. "If *you* lived here and six strangers showed up, wouldn't you react somehow? Come out to greet them? Shoot at them? Something?"

"Unless they're hidden," she said. "Unless they're afraid of us. Don't forget, they went to the trouble of shielding this place."

"There's always that," he agreed. And it *was* a real possibility. "But you don't believe that, do you? Not in your heart of hearts."

Troi returned his gaze. "I hate to say it, but . . ." She shook her head. "No. I don't. Whatever happened to the rest of the population must have happened here as well."

Riker sighed. "That's life, I guess. You win some, you lose some."

But he didn't stop walking. And neither did she.

"We're still going on?" she asked, just to confirm the fact.

"Yup. We've still got to check it out top to bottom," he said. "Those are our orders. Besides, we've come this far. It wouldn't make sense to turn back now."

Scott looked from one monitor to the other. The first one showed a graphic representation of the ion path they'd been following. The second displayed the section of the Dyson Sphere directly below them.

"This is the end of the rainbow," Geordi noted. He was intent on the monitor attached to the captain's seat.

"Aye," agreed Scott. "The end, all right."

"But still no pot of gold. No *Enterprise*."

Scott pointed to a detail on his monitor. "Look at the momentum distribution of the ions," he said. "It would take an impulse engine at full reverse to put out a signature like that."

"So wherever they went," Geordi said, picking up the line of reasoning, "they didn't go willingly. That makes sense. Tell you what . . . I'll search the surrounding space, you scan the surface of the sphere."

"Ye've got yerself a deal," the older man agreed.

As he worked, he shook his head. He still believed that the *Enterprise* had vanished inside the sphere; there was no other explanation. But if that was the case, how had it been accomplished? There was no visible means of entry . . . and without one, his theory—unlike the sphere—had a pretty big hole in it.

"Anything?" asked Geordi after a while.

Scott shrugged. "Some low-level radiation. And a lot of meteor debris." Suddenly, something caught his eye. "Wait," he said. "What's this?"

Homing in on a finite portion of the sphere, he brought up a sensor map. And sure enough, the surface of the thing wasn't as smooth and uninterrupted as it had first appeared.

"C'mere, lad," he told Geordi. "I've got something here ye might want to take a look at."

Moving to his side, the younger man peered over Scott's shoulder. "That circular line," he said. "It looks some kind of doorway. Or . . ." He paused. "Or an entry hatch!"

"Aye," Scott confirmed, vindicated. "Now look at this."

Working at his control board, he superimposed the image of the ion trail over the image of the hatch. The trail ended right above the circular line etched into the sphere. Scott and Geordi exchanged a look.

"I'll bet ye two bottles of scotch that the *Enterprise* is inside that sphere at this very moment," said Scott. "And that they went in right through that hatch."

"No bet here," said Geordi. "The question is . . . how do we get the door to open for *us?*"

Aye, thought Scott. That *was* a good question. Together, they examined the display for a moment. Then Geordi pointed to something.

"Look here. This appears to be some kind of communications array."

It looked familiar. "Aye," said the older man. "We found hundreds of them when we did our initial survey seventy-five years ago."

"Did you try hailing them?" asked Geordi.

"Sure. That was standard procedure in my day— nae that it did us any good. There was never any answer." He scowled. "And then the power coils blew up."

The younger man grunted. "Hailing is standard procedure today, too . . ." Suddenly, his face went taut with thought. "Wait a minute, Scotty. What if these *aren't* communications arrays? What if they're some kind of remote access terminals . . . that are triggered by subspace signals on certain frequencies?"

Scott felt a trickle of cold sweat run down his spine. "Frequencies like our standard ship's hail?"

"Exactly. When the *Enterprise* saw this terminal, they probably did the same thing you did seventy-five years ago—opened a channel. Only this time it triggered something that activated the hatch and pulled the ship inside the sphere."

Scott thought for a moment. "But why would the *Jenolen* nae have been pulled inside as well?" And then he answered his own question: "Ah. Because it was nae near a hatch."

"No," said Geordi, "it wasn't. But you might have activated a similar mechanism—one designed to *shunt* an incoming vessel to a hatch. Except . . . except maybe the *Jenolen* wasn't big enough or strong enough to survive the shunt, and its power coils bore the brunt of it."

The older man nodded admiringly. This Geordi La Forge had some promise after all. "A nice bit o' reasoning, laddie. Very nice indeed."

Geordi flashed a smile of thanks. But it faded a moment later, as he remembered the fix they were in.

"Let's assume for the moment that we're right," he told Scott. "How does that help us help the *Enterprise?* If we try to open the hatch, we might be pulled in like they were."

"Aye, lad. That's certainly somethin' to consider." And consider it he did.

Suddenly, it came to him. He snapped his fingers. "On the other hand . . . maybe all we need to do is get our *foot* in the door!"

Geordi was obviously puzzled. "Our . . . foot in the door?" he echoed. "I don't get it."

Suddenly feeling full of energy, Scott explained. "All right then, here it is. Y'see, we trigger the remote terminal with a subspace transmission . . ."

"Trigger it? But then, won't we be pulled in by whatever got the *Enterprise?*"

Scott shook his head. "Nae if we're far enough away—say a half million kilometers." He scratched at his jawline, playing out the scenario in his head. "Then, when the hatch starts to close again—wham! We rush in and use the *Jenolen* to jam the thing open until the *Enterprise* can escape."

Geordi looked at him as if the man had gone completely crackers. But Scott didn't mind. He was already moving toward his engineering consoles. After all, the sooner he got started, the sooner they could put their plan into action.

"You can't be serious," said the younger man, following him to the console. "That hatch . . . it could crush this ship like an egg—and a pretty fragile egg at that."

"Leave it to me," said Scott. "I can increase the shield strength by running warp power through the relay grid."

Geordi shook his head. "No way. These engines are barely holding together as it is. You push them too hard and they'll explode."

Scott shrugged off the possibility. "They'll hold, lad, don't ye worry about that. I know how to get a few extra gigawatts out o' these wee bairns."

Geordi sighed. "Scotty, this is suicide. I am not going to let you get us killed. There's got to be something else we can try. Something less . . . well, less *crazy.*"

But Scott would not be so easily denied. When he looked up at Geordi, his voice was a mixture of conviction and entreaty.

"Geordi, m'lad, I've spent my whole life figurin' out how to make crazy things work." His eyes fixed on the younger man's VISOR. "I'm telling ye—one engineer to another—I can *do* this."

For a moment, they looked at one another. Scott could almost see Geordi searching his heart and his instincts for a course of action. Finally, he made his decision.

"All right," he said. "Let's do it."

Grinning from one side of his face to the other, Scotty clapped him on the shoulder. "Attaboy, Mr. La Forge," he said with true affection. "Welcome to the club!"

And together, united in purpose, they turned their attention to what had to be done.

On the bridge of the *Enterprise,* Picard steeled himself against the impact of the onrushing solar flare. All around him, his officers did the same.

"Impact in twenty-two seconds," Worf announced.

The captain frowned. They had survived almost every manner of assault imaginable. They had weathered the most hideous of cosmic phenomena.

And here they were, virtually helpless in the face of a simple solar flare. It would be the ultimate irony if something so utterly commonplace accomplished what the Ferengi, the Romulans and the Borg had failed at: the destruction of Starfleet's premier vessel.

"Ten seconds," counted the Klingon.

Picard's teeth grated together. He refused to believe it would end this way. The *Enterprise* would survive, if by no other means than the force of her captain's will.

"Five," said Worf. "Four. Three. Two. One."

As the blossom of flaming plasma exploded against the cobbled-together shields of the *Enterprise,* the ship was shaken like a leaf in a windstorm. Picard held onto the edge of Data's console, barely keeping his feet.

But before that first split instant of impact had passed, he knew his ship had survived. And as he listened for Worf's voice, his conclusion was confirmed.

"Shields holding," the Klingon rumbled. "But down another fifteen percent, sir."

Damn. Another couple of flares like that one, thought Picard, and they'd be down to no shields at all. It was starting to look as if Data's prognosis— grim as it had sounded—was actually too optimistic.

Abruptly, the android turned to him. "Sir?" he said, asking for permission to speak.

What now? wondered the captain. *More bad news?* "Go ahead, Mr. Data."

"Helm control has been restored," his second officer reported. "Impulse power stands at sixty percent."

Picard smiled. "Excellent."

Under the circumstances, sixty percent sounded pretty good. Maybe their luck was finally changing.

"Ensign Rager," he said, "take us out of here at half-impulse. Double our distance from the star."

"Aye, sir," said Rager. "Three hundred thousand kilometers."

They'd reach their destination in seconds. And at that distance, the captain judged, they would be reasonably safe from the flares—even with their shields impaired.

Descending to Data's side, he added: "Now all we need is a way out of here."

The android looked up at him. "I could conduct a

search for another hatch or portal that might still be open."

"Good idea," remarked Picard. "Do so."

"However," Data went on, "the interior surface area of the sphere is more than ten to the sixteenth power square kilometers. It will take seven hours to completely scan the surface."

The ship shook again, though not as badly as before. Apparently, they were still in range of the flares. Picard glanced at the android meaningfully.

Data nodded. "I will endeavor to speed up the process," he promised.

"Thank you," said the captain. And as he turned his attention to the main viewscreen, he wondered how the away team was doing.

Chapter Thirteen

AS KANE WALKED alongside Sousa toward the next tower, he grunted. Something had tousled his hair. Turning in that direction, he felt a breeze. How about that? There was a wind coming up. Good. It would make this place seem like less of a tomb.

His fellow ensign seemed to take note of the wind, too. For a moment, their eyes met, and Kane saw the regret in Sousa's. But only for a moment, for after that he turned away, setting his sights on their destination.

It figured he'd end up being paired with Sousa, after what had happened between them. And it figured as well that he'd end up on this away team.

I finally get off the ship, he thought, and it turns out to be the most boring mission in the annals of Starfleet. He glanced at Riker, who was off on a parallel ramp toward another tower entirely. Thanks for nothing, Commander.

After Riker had finally conceded the uselessness of this mission, he'd split them up to get it over with that much faster. At least there was that, Kane told himself. At least it would be finished soon.

And then what? He didn't have much to look forward to back on the ship either. Unless, of course, his being included in this away team was an omen of things to come, and the first officer had finally decided to give him a break . . .

But first, there was this next tower. This *last* tower. Sighing with impatience, Kane followed a torturous bend in the ramp and walked up to the arched entranceway. Sousa was with him every step of the way. As if they were still buddies, still looking out for one another.

And whose fault was it that they were no longer buddies? Sousa's, by virtue of his pity? Or Kane's, by virtue of his humiliation?

It was one thing to hang out with people like Andy Sousa when you were riding high, and could feel good about throwing them a crumb. But when you were down, you didn't want to see them. You didn't want to be reminded of how far you'd fallen. And you certainly didn't want to accept pity from them, because pity was something *you* should be giving *them*—not the other way around.

So maybe it *was* his fault that he and Sousa were no longer friends. So what? Who cared?

As he pondered these things, they were engulfed by the tower. But it didn't take more than a second before Kane knew this one was like all the others. Lots of machines and nothing else.

Sousa seemed to have come to the same conclusion.

Kane could tell from the look in his eyes that he was ready to go. Suddenly, Kane found that he wanted to stay—at least for another few moments, if for no other reason than to be contrary.

And to be even more contrary, he took out his phaser. That got Sousa's attention, all right. It made his eyes open wide in the cool darkness of the tower.

"What are you doing?" he asked.

Kane shrugged. Using the business end of the phaser, he pointed to a bank of the builder race's machines. "Nothing much," he replied. "Just taking a closer look at these things—to see what's inside." And with that, he turned the weapon's setting selector up to the next-to-last position.

"No," said Sousa. "You're crazy."

"Maybe," Kane conceded. "Or maybe I'll find something in there that'll be the saving grace of this mission. And even if I don't—who's going to care? The people who built these things are deader than dust."

Without further ado, he trained his phaser on the nearest wall and activated it. A red beam lanced out into the midst of the alien machinery, creating a fist-sized pit of hissing vapor. The air in the tower was suddenly thick with the acrid scent of burning metal.

"Kane!" cried Sousa. "Stop, damn it! You don't know what you're messing around with!"

The ensign chuckled. "That's the whole point, helm-jockey. And what better way to find out what we're messing with . . . than to slit its belly and check out its entrails?"

As he raised the phaser's emitter, the line of seething vapor grew longer. And longer still. Of course, there wasn't a whole lot to see, other than black, twisted wires and pockets of what looked like broken glass, but that didn't keep Kane from continuing.

Whatever actual scientific curiosity he'd had about the machines was fading. They were now his chosen scapegoats—the objects on which he was focusing all the hatred and frustration that had been building up inside him.

"I said . . . cut it out!" bellowed Sousa over the hissing.

Kane ignored him. After all, what was he going to do about it? What—

Suddenly, the ensign felt something hard make contact with his jawbone. As the world went hot and red, he sprawled. And by the time he got control of his reeling senses, he found he was skidding backwards over the smooth alien floor.

Sousa was standing in the center of the tower, feet spread—as if he expected Kane to come back at him. And the phaser was scraping over the ground right next to its owner, having shut itself off when it left his hand.

As the ensign slid to a stop against the far wall, Kane noticed that something was wrong. Maybe it was the interplay of light and shadow, maybe something else. And by the time he realized *what* was wrong, it was too late to stop it.

With a horrible sound—like the cry of some great wounded beast—a wedge of alien machinery came tearing down off the wall. Kane saw Sousa wheel and look up at it, even try to escape it.

But he couldn't—not completely. The wedge hit him as it hit the floor, pinnning him beneath its awful weight.

Kane tried to say something, but the word wouldn't come out. And then, finally, he rasped: "Sousa!" And again, louder, so that it echoed in the lofty, alien edifice: "Sousaaa!"

Getting back on his feet, he scooped up his weapon and scrabbled over to his fallen comrade. Please be alive, he thought. Please be alive. And when he got there, his prayers were answered, because the man was still breathing.

But Sousa's left leg was caught underneath the section of machinery. Crushed, more than likely. And maybe he was hurt in other ways as well, because he wasn't opening his eyes.

Damn it, Kane told himself. What have I done? What have I done?

"Kane!" The cry came from behind him. Whirling, he saw Will Riker standing in the tower's arched entranceway.

"Commander!" the ensign called out, genuinely glad to see him. Hell, he needed help, didn't he? "It's Sousa! He's hurt!"

Scowling, the first officer crossed the intervening space in three strides and knelt at Sousa's side. Using his tricorder, he scanned the man's status.

"He's in shock," Riker concluded. "And losing blood." For the first time, he assessed the section of machinery. "We've got to get this off him."

"Sure," said Kane, eagerly grabbing one jagged side of the wedge. "Let's do it."

By that time, some help had arrived in the form of

Troi, Krause and Bartel. The Betazoid's features were twisted in agony, as if she herself had been the victim of the fallen weight. And the others were only slightly less anguished.

"My God," whispered Krause. "What happened here?"

But fortunately for Kane, there was no time to answer that question. They had to focus all their efforts on lifting the alien machinery.

"Ready," said Riker. "Heave!"

With an effort, they lifted the wedge—and as gently as she could, Troi pulled Sousa out from under it. Then they lowered the section to the ground again.

But Sousa looked terrible. His face was waxy, his hairline matted with sweat. Kane knelt at his friend's side as Troi scanned his leg with her tricorder. After all, she was the closest thing they had to a doctor on this away team.

"Is he . . . going to be all right?" asked Kane.

The counselor looked up at him . . . and her brows knit over her dark, soul-piercing eyes. She knows I'm responsible, thought the ensign. She can see the guilt twisting in my gut.

But she answered him anyway. "The bones in his leg have been crushed and there is some neurological damage. But nothing Dr. Crusher cannot fix."

Thank God, thought Kane. He's going to make it.

"That is," Riker added, "if we can get him back to the ship. Unfortunately, we can't just beam him back. We've got to bring him back by shuttle."

"But we cannot communicate with the shuttle through the shield," the Betazoid reminded him.

The first officer scowled. "And it's a long way back

to where we started—especially since we don't have a stretcher."

Troi shook her head. "Stretcher or no stretcher . . . I would prefer not to move him if there is another way. We must get the shuttle and pilot it here ourselves." Kane cursed inwardly. That would take a long time and Sousa was looking paler by the moment.

The first officer nodded. "Let's get started." He turned to Bartel. "Lieutenant, you're with—"

"Commander?" Kane had spoken before he knew it.

Riker looked at him. "Yes, Ensign?"

Kane swallowed. "Sir, I want to go with you. I want to . . ." What he meant to say was *to make up for what I did*. But his voice just trailed off.

The first officer misinterpreted the situation. "I understand. He's your friend." Turning to Bartel, he said, "Never mind."

Then, without even waiting to see if Kane was following him, Riker headed for the ramp. The ensign fell in right behind him.

This was going to be tricky, Geordi told himself. *Very* tricky.

Unfortunately, it wasn't as if they had a whole lot of choice in the matter. It was either try Scott's plan or let the *Enterprise* languish in its Dyson Sphere prison.

Moving on half-impulse power, the *Jenolen* crept nearer and nearer to the place where the hatch was supposed to be. If it *was* a hatch.

No, Geordi thought. No doubts. Not now.

He consulted his monitor. "We're at five hundred thousand kilometers," he told Scott.

At the next console over, his companion nodded. "Aye, lad." Playing the controls like a virtuoso, he brought the ship to a dead stop.

Geordi took a deep breath. Then, with the utmost concentration, he made the necessary preparations for their gamble. "How are the engines?" he asked.

"Engines are ready," Scott announced.

The younger man looked at him. Cool as a walk in the ether. Either Scott believed in his strategy a lot more strongly than Geordi did . . . or he was out of his mind. Or maybe a little bit of both.

"Okay," said La Forge. "Keep your fingers crossed. Here we go." Gritting his teeth, he sent them plunging toward the hatch.

Geordi's monitor showed the surface of the sphere. For a moment, nothing happened. Then slowly, miraculously, a crack opened. And kept opening.

He pumped his fist in the air. "All right!"

Scott harrumphed. "Ye dinnae have to sound so surprised," he remarked.

From around the circumference of the widening doorway, six spidery tractor beams reached up into space and searched for a ship. But they found nothing to latch onto, nothing to draw into their web.

"Come on," said Geordi. "There's nothing out there. Give it up." He held his fingers ready over his control panel. "I still can't open a channel to the *Enterprise,*" he told Scott. "There's too much interference. We'll have to wait until we're right in the doorway."

"That's all right, lad. We'll have time," his partner assured him.

The beams were persistent—but not persistent enough. After what seemed like a very long time, they finally shut off. A moment later, as if frustrated in its failure to swallow something, the hatch slowly began to slide closed.

"That's it," said Geordi, feeling his heart start to pump harder against his ribs. "Let's go! Full impulse power!"

Both of them worked their controls like madmen. Somewhere below their feet, the engines rumbled back into high gear. Would they hold up? Would the jury-rigged relay circuits? The power conduits?

As Geordi made a minute course correction, he found himself thinking about that auxiliary tank. It'd be a hell of a time for it to blow . . .

But seconds later, they were home free. They were speeding toward the hatch faster than it could shut them out—though the margin for error was still pretty thin. And thanks to his piloting, they were right on target.

As the opening diminished, they maneuvered the *Jenolen* into the middle of it . . . and then *stopped*. Geordi had time to glance at his partner in this mad venture. Scott was smiling. Actually smiling.

But then, Geordi told himself, his companion had already cheated death. To Montgomery Scott, every breath he had taken since leaving the *Jenolen*'s transporter was a bonus. And that made risking one's life a whole lot easier.

On the other hand, La Forge wasn't quite so willing

to give up the ghost. He'd "died" once before, and he knew it was no picnic.

"Any second now," said Scott, looking around—as if he could see the sphere's mechanical maw closing on them. "Any sec—"

Suddenly, the ship shuddered. The hatch had encountered the *Jenolen's* deflector shields. And just as Scott had predicted, their shields were stronger. They had indeed gotten their foot in the door.

But how long could they keep it there? Not wasting a second, Geordi opened a voice-communications channel to the *Enterprise*.

Chapter Fourteen

WORF HAD BEEN paying close attention to the communications monitor on his Tactical board, expecting to hear from Commander Riker and his away team. So when the screen lit up to indicate an incoming message, it was hardly cause for surprise.

Nonetheless, Worf *was* surprised. In fact, he could barely believe what his monitor was telling him; he had to look twice to confirm it.

"Captain," he said.

Picard, who'd been standing beside Data at Ops, turned around to acknowledge him. "Yes, Lieutenant?"

"There is an incoming audio message, sir."

The captain's forehead wrinkled. "Why didn't Commander Riker just contact me directly?"

Worf frowned. "It is *not* Commander Riker," he explained. "It is Commander *La Forge*, sir."

"La Forge . . . !" Picard's brows shot up. "By all means, Lieutenant, put him through!"

A moment later, Geordi's voice sang out on the tension-filled bridge. "This is Commander La Forge. Do you read me, *Enterprise*?"

"We read you, Commander," the captain assured him. "Go ahead, Geordi."

Geordi hung on to one of the engineering consoles in the *Jenolen*. The ship was shaking like crazy, its shields threatening to buckle on them, its overworked engines roaring to beat the band—despite Scotty's best efforts.

As he spoke to Captain Picard, Geordi tried to ignore the chaos around him. He had to accomplish what he and his companion had set out to accomplish: the rescue of the *Enterprise*.

"Captain, we're using the *Jenolen* to hold open the hatch at the entrance to the sphere . . ."

"What?" exclaimed Picard. "Did I hear you correctly, Commander?"

"You did, sir. But our shields won't stand the pressure much longer."

There was the briefest of pauses. "Understood," came the captain's reply. "Unfortunately, we cannot return to the entrance just yet. Commander Riker and an away team are down on the surface."

Scott cried out. "They're bleedin' *where?*"

Great, thought Geordi. *Just great.*

"I cannot leave without them," Picard said grimly.

"And I can't make any promises," he told the captain. "But we'll hold out as long as we can. La Forge out."

* * *

"Damn," said Riker, raising his voice to be heard. "Where did this wind come from?"

Kane, who was right behind him, shook his head to show he had no answer either. When they'd left the tower in which Sousa and the others were sheltered, the ensign had noticed that the breeze was much brisker. But it had been nothing like this.

If the ramps had been silent on the way in, they were hardly that now. The same gusts that buffeted them, forcing them to keep low to the surface or be pushed backward, seemed to spur entire flights of demonic howls from the depths of the chasms beneath them.

Fortunately, they had almost reached the beam-down site at the outskirts of the sensor-shielded area. Another hundred yards or so, maybe less, and they'd be able to contact the ship. What's more, there was a tower between them and their destination—a place to rest and catch their breath.

Kane was glad they didn't have to go back for their companions. In this wind, it would be nearly impossible. They would just take refuge in one of the towers —the one up ahead or some other—and wait for the shuttle to arrive.

Unlike people, a shuttle could handle weather like this, he told himself. They were built to withstand adverse conditions.

The concept of human fragility put him in mind of Sousa's injury. How could he have been so stupid? How could he have just blasted away at those alien machines?

Kane wished he had it all back again. He wished he could rewind it and erase it, as if it had never really happened in the first place. But he couldn't, could he? No matter how well Sousa healed, no matter what else took place, he'd always have to live with the knowledge of what he'd done.

And he wouldn't be the only one. Troi knew too— maybe not down to the last detail, but she knew. And she wasn't going to keep it a secret—not something as serious as almost getting somebody killed on an away mission.

What's more, Kane didn't blame her. Whatever he got, he deserved.

Suddenly, the tower was right ahead of them. And as they pressed forward into its shadow, it shielded them from the wind to a certain degree. Tired and sore from their exertions, they lurched into the arched entranceway and took seats on the floor just inside.

Riker shook his head, his face red and windburned. "Nice weather we're having."

The ensign grunted—then turned away, as if sizing up the last stretch ahead of them. After what he'd done, he couldn't look the man in the eye.

Riker seemed not to notice. Sighing, he got to his feet again. "Come on," he said. "No rest for the weary, Ensign."

Following the first officer's example, Kane stood and made his way out onto the outgoing ramp. After his brief respite, the wind hit him with what seemed like even greater ferocity. Worse, it appeared to have gotten temperamental; it was shifting directions now, making it harder to keep his balance.

Alternately shuffling forward in the crosswinds and plunging forward when they momentarily abated, the ensign made good progress. But up ahead, Riker was plowing through at a much better clip. Maybe where he came from, Kane speculated, people were used to this kind of weather.

Suddenly, before his disbelieving eyes, the first officer was knocked right off his feet by an unexpectedly powerful gust. Nor did it stop there. Even as Riker clawed at the surface of the ramp, it slid him quickly and without warning to the very brink.

Kane tried to forge ahead with greater speed, to lend a hand, but it was no use; he couldn't make enough headway. He'd barely gone a half-dozen steps before Riker slipped over the edge and was gone.

"Noooo!" he cried, the wind tearing at the word as soon as it left his mouth. "Damn it, nooo!"

First Andy Sousa, and now Will Riker. Both victims of his foolishness. If not for his itchy trigger finger, they could all be huddled safe and sound in some tower. Instead, the first officer was dead—and maybe his friend would be too, before long.

All my fault, thought Kane. *Mine.*

And then he saw a hand still clutching at the edge of the ramp where Riker had gone over. Five fingers that were clinging to life, but slowly losing their grip . . .

Diving forward, oblivious to the chance that he'd be blown over the side as well, the ensign landed a meter or so short of Riker's hand. "Hang on!" he cried, not sure at all that the man could hear him. "Hang on!"

Crawling forward on his belly, he ignored the crosswind that tore at him, trying to shove him in the wrong direction. His world, the entire universe, had come down to only one thing: saving his commanding officer.

Inch by inch, he pulled himself forward. Inch by

inch, he fought the winds, the slickness of the ramp and his own fatigue. And at last, after what seemed like forever, he was within striking distance.

By then, Riker's fingers were white, and only a knuckle away from oblivion. Kane reached out and grabbed for the spot where the man's wrist should have been. As he'd hoped, there was something there; he closed his hand on it . . .

Just as Riker lost his grip. Kane felt a terrible weight threaten to wrench his arm out of its socket as the first officer dangled free in the vicious air currents. Then, as he lay helpless to do anything about it, he found himself slipping slowly toward the edge.

Something inside him screamed for him to let Riker go. Otherwise, they'd *both* go over and be lost in the chasm below. They'd *both* die.

But Kane wasn't buying it. He hung on, his cheek pressed flat against the smooth surface, even as the first officer's weight dragged him to the very limit of the ramp. He could almost feel himself gliding over it into the maw of infinity . . .

But he didn't. He stopped right there. And a moment later, Riker began climbing his arm. When he felt a viselike grip just below his elbow, he let go of the first officer's wrist—and then felt another grip above his bicep.

Before he knew it, Riker had climbed up his arm and clamped a hand on the ramp again. A second later, his other hand joined it. Without a weight to pull him down, Kane was able to grab at the front of the other man's tunic. And together, with one enormous effort, they dragged the first officer up out of death's dark domain.

For a time, they just lay there on the rampway, gasping—stripped to their barest emotions. Then Riker took the ensign by the shoulder and pulled him along toward the beam-down site.

Kane couldn't believe the man's courage. He'd been swinging in the wind a moment ago, so close to oblivion he could've reached out and touched it. And he still could find the wherewithal to push on—to complete his mission.

Half-walking, half-crawling, they closed the gap. Even before they reached the circular plate on which they'd materialized, the first officer tapped his communicator and called out the captain's name.

Luck was with them. "Number One—are you all right? What's all that noise in the background?" asked Picard.

Riker told him. He told him about Sousa, too.

"You'd better hurry," said the captain. In the next few moments, he explained about the *Jenolen* and the *Enterprise*'s chance to escape the sphere. "We'll hold out as long as we can," he promised. "But we haven't got much time."

Picard's imperative was still echoing in Kane's head when he saw his companion tap his communicator again.

"Riker to shuttle," he bellowed.

"Shuttlecraft *LaSalle* responding," Riker's communicator replied.

As Kane looked up, he saw something he didn't like—not at all. "Commander—look!"

The ensign pointed to the shuttle, which was rocking violently in the heavy winds. It was no longer where they'd left it. It was now only meters away from one of the towers.

The first officer cursed.

"Two to beam up," he told the shuttle, "now."

But before the craft could comply, a mighty gust did just what they'd feared: it smashed the *LaSalle* into the alien edifice. Hard.

A moment later there was a titanic explosion. Kane could feel the heat of it on his face. And just like that, the shuttle was gone—in its place, a shower of flaming debris.

The ensign's heart sank, but Riker didn't miss a beat. "We've got to alert the others," he said. "We've got to tell them to come on ahead as best they can." He paused grimly. "And then hope that the *Enterprise* can beam us up on her way out of here."

"Riker to Counselor Troi!" The first officer shouted.

No answer.

He tried it again.

Still nothing.

"It's the sensor shield," said Riker. It doesn't just stop signals from above. It stops signals *underneath* it as well."

The ensign nodded. "You're right," he said. "It's useless."

And that left only one alternative. Kane flinched inwardly at the thought of it. He glanced back the way they'd come . . . at the zagging, wind-torn ramps and the howling chasms. Then he looked at Riker.

"You stay here," said the first officer. "I'll go back and get them!"

The ensign was tempted to let him have his way. At

least for a second or two. And then he grabbed Riker's tunic again—just as he had a little while ago.

"The hell you will," he roared. "I'm coming too!"

The first officer glared at him. And then, gradually, a smile spread over his face.

"Have it your way," he bellowed. "Just don't get into any trouble, all right?"

Kane nodded. "You've got my word on it!"

Screwing up their nerve, they started back for Sousa and the others.

Chapter Fifteen

DEANNA TROI HAD BEGUN to worry when she heard the winds outside their tower howling like banshees. Leaving Sousa in the hands of Bartel and Krause, she had gone over to the arched entrance through which Riker and Kane had departed and felt the force of the weather on her face.

She had said a single word, a name: *"Will . . ."*

He was in danger. She didn't need a communicator to discover that; she could tell by the ebb and flow of his emotions. Terrible danger. And yet, she couldn't lift a hand to help him.

Now, she stood by the entranceway again—no longer afraid, but confused. The winds were still yowling, though perhaps they were starting to die down a bit.

And Will Riker was still alive—despite that awful moment when it had seemed he would perish. Even at a distance, she could sense his presence, vital, determined. And he'd certainly been gone long enough to get the shuttle. More than long enough.

So the shuttle should be on its way, she told herself. And Will, along with that guilt-ridden Ensign Kane, should be in it.

But they weren't. They were headed back the way they'd come—on foot. Something had gone wrong.

The shuttle was never going to arrive. Frowning, she looked back at Sousa and the two engineers. They were going to have to carry the injured man to the beam-down site, weren't they?

Just as she thought that, Troi scanned the expanse of alien architecture again—and saw two figures on one of the ramps leading to their tower. Two men in red and black.

"My god," whispered a voice behind her. Turning, she saw Bartel. Normally the picture of efficiency, the woman looked shaken. "You were right, Counselor. They're coming back without the shuttle."

Minutes later, Riker and Kane came lurching into the tower. Both of them were out of breath, and their eyes were swollen from staring down the wind.

"No shuttle," Krause said, just for the record.

"No shuttle," the first officer confirmed. He was tired and he was breathing too hard. "We're going to have to reach the beam-down site on our own—and *fast*. Geordi's managed to use the *Jenolen* to wedge the hatch open, but it won't hold up in there forever."

Troi nodded. "So what are we waiting for?" she asked. "Let's do it."

Riker regarded the ensign and the two engineers.

"You heard the counselor. If we each grab a limb, we can make it."

"And what about me?" Troi inquired.

The first officer looked at her, his face rubbed raw by his battle with the weather. "You replace the first one that falls," he said.

On the bridge of the *Enterprise*, Captain Picard listened to the bad news. "Five more minutes," he echoed.

"At best," shouted Geordi, straining to be heard over the grinding of the *Jenolen*'s engines. "Maybe not even *that* long."

Picard nodded. Time was running out. But his chief engineer had been careful to restrict his comments to the status of the transport ship—and not to offer any advice as to the fate of the away team.

Only a captain could make the decision to leave a team behind—to sacrifice the few for the sake of the many. And if Picard refused to make that decision, neither Geordi nor anyone else could make it for him.

Come on, Will, he thought, silently encouraging his first officer. *Don't make me be the one to sign your death warrant.*

A bloody-shirted Kane held Andy Sousa's injured leg —the one the alien machinery had all but crushed —as he made his way through the winds of the long-dead Dyson Sphere world. Beside him, Riker held Sousa's good leg, and up ahead, Krause and Bartel led the way. Each of them held one of Sousa's shoulders; they took turns supporting his head.

Every now and then, the ensign glanced at his friend's face. It looked ruddy, but that was the effect of the weather. Beneath that deceptive glow, Sousa was hanging onto his life by a thread.

Some time ago, Kane had lost the feeling in his hands, but he refused to ask for help. Krause and Bartel had each been replaced by Counselor Troi at least once since they left the tower, but he was determined she wouldn't replace *him*.

After all, he was the one who'd gotten them into this mess. He wasn't going to let anyone else carry his rightful load.

Fortunately, the gusts had diminished somewhat in their intensity. Or at least he thought they had. The crosswinds were still vicious, still eager to tear them sideways off the ramps—but the team seemed to be making good headway despite them.

"Look!" cried the empath suddenly. She was pointing up ahead.

Kane had no perspective on how far they'd come. He'd been too intent on keeping his footing and not dragging the others down with him. But as he looked up now, following Troi's gesture, his heart leaped.

They were almost at the last tower. And just past that was the beam-down site. Now if only they'd made it in time . . .

With renewed determination, they forged ahead. The tower seemed to loom larger and larger still, until they were almost on top of it. Then they were inside, and the winds were silent, if only for the briefest of moments.

They didn't have the luxury of resting up, of gathering themselves for that last stretch of rampway between them and their goal. They had to push on if they were to make their deadline.

And push on they did, the wind like a fist in his face. Kane's muscles fairly screamed from his exertions—especially those he'd used to pull Commander Riker back from certain death—but he gritted his teeth and did his best to ignore the pain. It would all be over soon enough, he promised himself. It would be over in a few steps . . . and a few more . . . and a few more . . .

Then, as if in a dream, he heard someone shouting. At *him?* He forced his puffy, wind-scoured eyes to focus—and saw Commander Riker, thundering at the top of his lungs.

But not at Kane. He was hollering at the heavens. And his hand—little more than a claw now—was pressed tightly to his communicator emblem.

The ensign looked around . . . and wanted to cry. They'd reached the ramp that led to the beam-down site. They'd *made* it.

Now all they had to do was get through to the ship. The hatch wasn't far from here. The *Enterprise* would probably have to pass within transporter range on its way out of the sphere. Unless . . . unless the ship had already left without them. That was possible, wasn't it? No matter how badly the captain had wanted to retrieve them, he couldn't risk the lives of everyone else on board if the chance to escape was slipping from their grasp.

For a moment, Kane pondered the prospect of remaining in the sphere. Of wandering from tower to tower in a futile search for food and water until their legs couldn't support them anymore . . . of being forced to haunt this strange, sterile place along with all its other ghosts.

Then he heard a familiar voice wafting in the savage winds: "Acknowledged, Number One! We're on our way!"

The ensign looked at Andy Sousa—and as if the injured man had heard Picard's voice too, he opened his eyes. For a second or two, he gazed at Kane, trying to get the man to stay in focus.

"Damn," said Kane. "I'm sorry, Andy. I really am."

Sousa didn't say anything in return. He didn't have the strength. But at least he wasn't glaring at him. Maybe later he'd remember what happened and hate him like crazy. But for now, it was all right.

Kane found that he had a lump in his throat—a big one. He closed his eyes, not wanting to show the emotion there. If only they would get on with the damned transport already, he told himself. If only . . .

And then he realized that the winds had stopped howling. Opening his eyes, he saw that they were standing on a transporter platform. As a squad of medical personnel rushed up to take Sousa off their hands, the ensign spotted Captain Picard at the far end of the room, next to Chief O'Brien.

Once he was certain that the away team had arrived in one piece, the captain tapped his communicator. "Picard to the bridge."

"Aye, sir?" came the reply. It sounded like Commander Data.

"We've got them," the captain said. "Let Geordi know we're on our way."

Kane turned to a haggard, hollow-eyed Riker. "Will that be all, sir?" he rasped.

The first officer clapped him on the shoulder. "Yes, Ensign. That'll be all."

"Thank you, sir," said Kane. After all, he hadn't wanted to lose consciousness while he was still on duty. But since he was on his own time now, he fainted dead away.

"Commander La Forge?"

Geordi looked down at his communications panel. He knew that voice.

"What is it, Data?"

"I have been asked to tell you: We have recovered Commander Riker's team. We are on our way to the entrance now."

The engineer let out a breath. "That's good, Data. Another minute and—"

Suddenly, one of the panels in the Ops center exploded, bathing both Geordi and Scott in a rain of white-hot sparks. Before the younger man knew it, Scott was rushing over to check the damage.

"Damn!" he cried. "The plasma intercooler's gone. She's overheatin'!"

Working at his console to contain the problem, Geordi muttered a curse of his own. "I've lost helm control!"

"Geordi? Are you all right?" the android asked.

Geordi shook his head, forgetting that there was no way Data could see him. "I've been better!" he cried.

A second panel blew out, and then a third. Both of them burst into flame. They were losing the battle—and on the verge of losing the war.

"We've reached our limit," said Scott, "and passed it. There's no way we're going to get the ship out of here now! Tell 'em!"

Geordi pounded on his useless control console. His partner was right. No matter what, they were stuck here—until the hatch destroyed their shields and crushed them like a walnut.

"Mr. La Forge!" It was the captain he heard now. "What is your status?"

"Lousy," he cried. "We won't be able to move the *Jenolen* out of the way when you arrive."

"What are you saying?" asked Picard. His voice was breaking up now; even the communications system was going to pieces.

Gagging on the smoke that was filling the Ops center at an alarming rate, Geordi barked: "What I'm saying is *this* . . . you're going to have to destroy the *Jenolen* in order to get out of there!"

Absorbing La Forge's bleak message, Picard turned to his second officer. "Mr. Data . . . how long will it take us to reach them?"

"With our impulse engines operating at sixty percent power," said the android, "it will take one minute forty seconds to reach the entrance."

Captain Scott's voice came over the communications link, strident with urgency. "I cannae hold her together any longer, sir. Ye've got maybe two minutes before the engines go critical—*tops!*"

Picard spoke to the intercom grid. He'd sent Riker

down to engineering, to expedite things if he could. "This is the captain. I need more speed, Commander."

"Aye, sir," came the answer. "We're on it, sir!"

Picard felt his fists clenching. Despite Riker's optimistic response, there was only so much he could do down there. It was going to be close—too close.

"Bridge to Transporter Room Three," he said. "Stand by to beam two from the *Jenolen* as soon as we're in range."

"Aye, Captain," replied O'Brien. "Standing by!"

On the viewscreen, the starfield faded . . . turned blue, with a hint of green. Abruptly, the *Enterprise* was plummeting through the atmosphere, heading for the distant escape hatch.

Once again, their diminished shield capacity left them open to rising temperatures from the friction of "reentry"—but not so much as when they had no shields at all. Besides . . . what other choice did they have?

Picard glanced at Worf. "Load photon torpedoes," he commanded.

"Photon torpedoes loaded and locked on target," the Klingon barked.

On the *Jenolen,* everything was falling apart. The ship was shaking badly. Consoles were sparking and exploding. The lighting was flickering and the engine noise was a shriek of overworked metal.

Scott had been called a miracle worker in his day. But he'd just run out of miracles. Turning to La Forge, he shouted over the din.

"She's coming apart, lad! I cannae do anything more for her!"

The younger man looked at him, sweat streaming down both sides of his face. He managed a smile, even now. "I know, Scotty. I know."

What else could he say? They'd fought the good fight. They'd done their best. They'd even come close.

But in the end, Scott reflected bitterly, they'd *lost*.

Chapter Sixteen

Picard saw Data turn to glance over his shoulder at him. "We are within transporter range, sir."

The captain felt as if he had been waiting for that cue forever. Without a moment's hesitation, he said: "Bridge to transporter room! Energize!" And then to Worf, almost in the same breath: "Fire torpedoes, Lieutenant!"

"Aye, sir!" called the Klingon, executing as quickly as he possibly could. After all, there was no margin for error. If he got his barrage off even a split second too late, they'd hit the *Jenolen* and go up in the biggest conflagration this strange world had ever known.

Picard watched the forward viewscreen as the transport ship—still caught in the hatchway of the Dyson Sphere—loomed larger and larger, bathed in bright splashes of phaser fire. But even then, the plucky

Jenolen refused to succumb, refused to yield to the atom-shredding blasts.

For a terrible, gut-wrenching instant, the captain was certain they weren't going to destroy the ship in time. He was certain they were going to plow into her, destroying both vessels and all their occupants.

Fortunately, he was wrong. In a sudden blaze of glory, the *Jenolen* exploded. But they weren't out of danger yet—far from it.

Because as soon as the *Jenolen* was out of the way, the jaws of the hatch had begun to come together again. And though the *Enterprise* was hurtling toward the opening as fast as its damaged engines could propel it, the aperture was already pitifully small.

Would they make it? Would they get there before the hatch closed, trapping them inside again—perhaps forever?

Picard's eyes narrowed as he watched their window of opportunity dwindle. By his reckoning, the *Enterprise* was already too wide to get through.

"Helm," he cried, "roll to port—ninety degrees!"

The image on the viewscreen rotated ninety degrees in the opposite direction. The captain's estimate had been a good one; they were now in a position to slip through the ever-narrowing egress.

Holding his breath, Picard concentrated on the sliver of star-strewn space that beckoned from beyond their escape hatch—knowing full well it might be the last thing he ever saw. After all, they had long ago given up the option of turning back. And if they didn't hit their mark in time, they would dash their lives out on the sphere's superhard inner skin.

Close they came, closer still . . .

And then, before he knew it, before he could even *begin* to believe it, the splinter of an opening was gone. It had been replaced by a familiar sight: that of the sprawling galaxy in all its star-pricked splendor.

Exhaling, the captain pulled down on his uniform front and turned to Data: "Rear view, Commander."

As the android complied, the viewscreen showed them the dark, foreboding surface of the Dyson Sphere—once again flawless, once again unperturbed. And best left that way, Picard thought.

Suddenly, he remembered: Geordi. Captain Scott.

"You've got the conn," he told Data. And without a word of explanation, he headed for the transporter room.

"Come on," growled Chief O'Brien, laboring at his controls. "After all you've been through, you can't give up now. Damn it, you can't!"

As if either of his charges had any voice in whether they came back to the *Enterprise* alive—or remained on the *Jenolen* in the form of biological debris. As if it wasn't, finally and irrevocably, up to *him*—Mrs. O'Brien's boy Miles.

Across the room, up on the transporter platform, the outlines of two men flickered hopefully. A grim O'Brien set his teeth. He had a chance. They were out there somewhere, if only he could reel them in.

Abruptly, the shimmering outlines disappeared. O'Brien's heart sank. But he'd done this enough times to know that there was still a chance. Making adjustments in the attitude of the emitter array, he tried to bring them back again.

A moment later, they reappeared—but they were

still flickering. This was going to be a fight all the way. Ever so carefully, he modulated the gain in the phase transition coils and sent more power to the pattern buffer.

The images got stronger. And stronger still. He could almost make out details in their clothing, even in their faces. One of them was wearing a VISOR, he noted.

Still, the transporter chief had to be careful. After all, he'd captured a whole lot of molecules that were neither Geordi nor Scott, and it would take some doing to separate those out. If he got too eager, if he failed to bring them out of the buffer at just the right frequency . . . he didn't even want to think about it.

"Steady now," he told himself. "Slow and steady does it."

Finally, the outlines stabilized. They took on texture. And then, as if their atoms hadn't been travelling through space a few seconds ago at a speed that could barely be imagined, the two men materialized.

For a moment, they just stood there, amazed that they were still alive. Then they looked at each other. And they *laughed,* despite everything. Or was it *because* of everything?

Scott threw an arm around La Forge's shoulder. "There now," he said. "That was nae so bad, was it?"

Geordi smiled back at him. "I guess it could've been worse," he said judiciously. "Although I think I've had one close transport too many."

Scott's eyes opened wide. *"You?* How about *me?* If I never *see* another transporter, it'll be too soon."

And like a couple of drunken sailors, they staggered off the platform together. O'Brien watched them go—hearing their banter rise to a crescendo as they saw a familiar face out in the corridor—until the doors closed behind them.

Shaking his head and chuckling, he said: "You're welcome, lads. Pleased to be of service."

At the sound of her door chimes, Deanna Troi turned away from her desktop monitor. She hadn't been expecting anyone . . .

But then, she was the ship's counselor. And people's problems didn't stick to a regimented schedule.

"Come in," she said.

A moment later, the door slid aside. Ensign Kane was standing in the opening, looking more than a little uncomfortable—even hesitating for a bit before taking her up on her invitation to come inside.

The Betazoid smiled. "Sit down, Mr. Kane." And then, after he'd taken a seat: "What can I do for you?"

Not that she had any doubt about why he was here. This had to be about what had happened on the away mission.

But Kane didn't talk about it. Not directly—not yet. "I just visited Ensign Sousa," he said. "He's sleeping now, but he's going to be all right."

"Yes," she replied. "I know. I have been to see him too."

"He certainly gave us a scare," the young man noted.

"That he did," Troi agreed.

Kane cleared his throat. "Uh, back in that tower . . ." he began. "The one where the wedge of machinery fell on Ensign Sousa?"

"Yes," she said. "I remember."

Kane straightened. "That machinery didn't just come off the wall. I, uh . . . I shot it off with my phaser." He licked his lips. "Accidentally, of course. But it was me all the same."

"I see," said the Betazoid. "Have you told this to anyone else?"

"No," he responded. "You're the first. Because you've got a pretty good idea of what happened already, I think. And . . . because it's easier than telling Commander Riker."

Troi met the young man's gaze. "But don't you think he knows?"

Kane looked shocked. "Commander Riker? How would he . . . ?"

"Simple," said the counselor. "He got a look at the machinery. He saw the edge, with its burnt components." She shook her head. "Only a phaser beam— or something very much like it—could have created an edge like that."

The ensign swallowed. "I see," he said. "Then maybe I should go to see him after all. Anyway, you probably don't accept resignations."

Troi feigned bewilderment—although she had read his emotional state like an open book. "Resignations? Are you saying you intend to quit Starfleet?"

Kane nodded. "Yes. I mean, it's not as if I have much of a choice, right? Sooner or later, Andy's going to tell everyone what happened, and—"

"I don't think he will do that," the empath interjected. "He is your friend, after all."

"He *was* my friend," the ensign amended.

"No," Troi maintained. *"Is.* I am an empath, remember? I know Mr. Sousa pretty well. He will not get you in trouble."

Kane grunted, perhaps a little surprised. "Even so," he said, "I did it. You know it. Commander Riker knows it. And I know it."

The counselor leaned back in her chair. "I do not think Commander Riker is going to get you in trouble, either. He has already filed his report—and there was no mention of your using your phaser in it."

The ensign grunted again. This time, he was definitely surprised. "Really," he said.

"Really," she confirmed. "I believe he took into account some of the other things you did down there. For instance, your volunteering to accompany him back to the beam-down site. The way you persevered, despite the high winds, and saved his life. And not least, the way you went back again for Mr. Sousa, when you could have stayed where you were."

Kane thought about it. "You mean . . . he forgives me?"

"Something like that," Troi agreed. "And if *he* forgives you, who am I to do otherwise?"

The ensign shook his head. "I thought Commander Riker hated me," he muttered.

The Betazoid smiled. "Commander Riker can be a tough man to please," she conceded. "If he doesn't like your attitude, he lets you know it—in a variety of ways. But hate?" She chuckled softly. "The only thing he hates is failing to bring out the best in someone."

Kane pondered that for a moment. "Well, he sure had a challenge in me." A pause. "I'm not exactly the nicest person on the ship, Counselor."

She shrugged. "Nice is as nice does," she said. "And I cannot think of anything more altruistic than putting your life on the line for someone else."

The ensign grunted. For the first time since he'd come in, there was a hint of a smile on his face. "Me—an altruist," he said, as if trying it on for size. "That's not the kind of person my father used to tell me to be. His philosophy was every man for himself— and the devil take the hindmost."

"Not exactly an *enlightened* philosophy," Troi noted.

"I guess not," Kane agreed. "I see that now." Suddenly, he grew sober again. "But none of this changes what happened—what I did to Mr. Sousa."

The counselor leaned forward in her chair. "We all make mistakes, Ensign. Fortunately, yours is not irrevocable. If I were you, I would put it behind me . . . and start fresh. Besides," she told him, "Commander Riker has put a great deal of work into you. Both he and I would be reluctant to see it go to waste."

Her visitor seemed to accept that. "I'll have to think about it some more," he said.

"You do that," she replied encouragingly. But she thought she knew what his decision would be.

Kane stood. "In any case, I've got a lot of apologizing to do. For the way I acted . . . for the things I said. Starting with Commander Riker . . . and Captain Picard . . ." He swore softly. "And Captain Scott, as well."

"Captain Scott?" asked Troi.

The ensign nodded. "He came into the shuttlebay to admire the vehicles. And I called security on him."

The empath suppressed a giggle. "I see."

"There was one shuttle in particular," Kane recalled. "One he really seemed to take a shine to. The *Christopher,* I think it was." He looked up at her. "Man . . . if it was up to me, I'd *give* him that ship."

Troi smiled. "An admirable thought," she said. "You see? You *can* be nice."

The ensign grunted. "Yeah. Well, thanks for your help, Counselor."

"Think nothing of it," she told him. "It is my job."

Taking a deep breath, Scott activated the computer terminal in his quarters. There was no point in avoiding it anymore, he told himself. He could've died on the *Jenolen* never knowing the truth. And he owed it to himself—to *them*—to find out.

One by one, he brought up their names, the names of those with whom he'd risked his life time and again. One by one, he queried the *Enterprise*'s computer as to their status, their whereabouts. And one by one, the computer supplied the answers.

Not all the answers were happy ones. Death had laid claim to some, though none of them had died any way but proudly. He took solace in that.

Besides, he had expected some bad news. Time hadn't stood still for them the way it had for him. There were bound to have been some casualties in seventy-five long years; not every ship returned to port. Not every person survived, or was accounted for.

But some of them had lived and done well for themselves. McCoy, for example, had become an admiral. Who would have predicted that? Of all of them, he'd been the one most opposed to Starfleet's bureaucracy—and here he'd gone and become part of it.

Then there was Spock. First a respected ambassador, just like his father. And recently, a force for the reunification of Vulcan and Romulus—now working in secret for the same cause. It was just like Spock to take on the most impossible task he could find. And knowing him, he'd be equal to it.

So it went. Scott perused the files once, twice, a third time. Before he was done, he'd all but memorized them. And he'd gone from gladness to sorrow and back again so many times that he felt like a Ping-Pong ball.

Finally, he'd had enough. Storing the last of the biographical details, Scott sat back in his chair and sighed. He felt as if he'd been in a brawl and lost—badly—but he had no regrets. He knew he'd done the right thing.

Montgomery Scott had made his peace with his past. Only now he could think about facing his future.

Epilogue

GEORDI GRINNED as Scott made the turbolift compartment echo with his enthusiasm.

" 'But how did ye do it?' the captain asks me. And I tell him: 'Sir, I just had the cleanup detail pile every last one of those wee beasties onto the transporter platform.' And he looks at me, sort of horrified—sort of the way ye're looking now, lad—and says: 'But Scotty . . . ye did nae just transport them out into space, did ye?' "

Geordi looked at him. "Well . . . did you?"

"What do ye think? Of course nae. So I put on an offended expression, something like *this,* an' I say, 'I'm a kindhearted man, sir. I gave them a good home.' And the captain says, 'Where, man? Spit it out now!' And I tell him that I gave them to the *Klingons.* Just before they went into warp, I transported the whole kit and kaboodle into their *engine room*—as a wee parting gift!"

The younger man shook his head. "You didn't!"

Scott placed his hand over his heart. "May I be struck by lightnin' if I've changed a single word of it!"

The turbolift doors opened and Geordi ushered him out. "All right," he said. "Now I've got one for you."

As they started down the corridor, he related—in broad strokes, of course—the most preposterous story he could think of. It felt good to be telling Scotty a tall tale, instead of the other way around.

"Come on now," said his companion. "Ye're pullin' an old man's leg!"

"No, really," Geordi insisted. "This alien space baby—which was about the size of a four-story building—really thought the *Enterprise* was its mother."

"So what'd ye do?" asked Scotty.

The younger man rubbed his hands together. "Well," he said, "it was suckling power directly from the ship's fusion reactors. So Doctor Brahms and I—"

"Doctor Brahms?" repeated Scotty. "And who's that?" He winked. "Someone special, I'd wager, by the way ye said her name."

Geordi blushed. "She's married. And besides, that's another story entirely. Anyway, we changed the power frequency from twenty-one centimeters to point-oh-two centimeters . . ."

Scotty had already caught on. "Ye soured the milk, did ye?"

"That's right," Geordi confirmed. "How did you know?"

His companion shrugged. "They say that great minds think alike. And I ask ye now, who am I to argue with 'em?"

They laughed at that. But just seconds later, Scott's smile seemed to fade a bit. He put his hand on Geordi's shoulder.

"Ye know," he said, "in a way, I envy you."

"Envy me?" replied La Forge. "You're the one who's a living legend."

Scott shook his head. "It's always better to be on yer way than arrivin'," he declared. "The journey's always sweeter than its end."

"Come on," Geordi told him. "Don't go all nostalgic on me now."

The older man shrugged. "Enjoy these times, Geordi. Ye're the chief engineer of a starship. It's a time of yer life that'll never come again. And once it's gone, it's gone for good."

The engineer of the *Enterprise*-no-suffix took his hand back and sighed. As he looked ahead, a slight frown crossed his face. "Not that retirement is so bad," he commented. "I hear the Norpin Five colony is very . . . er, quiet this time o' year."

Geordi stopped in front of the shuttlebay doors. Scott stopped too, a little surprised.

"I thought ye were going to buy me a drink in Ten-Forward," he said. "Dinnae tell me ye're withdrawin' yer offer."

The younger man smiled. "I changed my mind."

Indicating the doors, which slid aside at his approach, he led the way into the shuttle bay. Consumed with curiosity, Scott followed.

He wasn't disappointed, either. Not a single bit.

Picard, Riker, Worf, Dr. Crusher, Troi and Data were all standing beside a large, gleaming shuttlecraft. On its side, in an elegant, flowing script, there was but one word. A name: *Christopher*.

The craft's space door was open. Stunned, Scott looked it over, then glanced back at his friends.

"Does this mean what I think it means?"

Riker chuckled. "That all depends on what you think it means."

"For instance," said Picard, "if you think it means we're making a gift of it to you . . ."

"Then you are correct," Worf finished.

The captain looked at him, a little taken aback at his enthusiasm.

The Klingon straightened. "Sorry, sir."

Scott shook his head. "Ye're going to give me one of your shuttles?" For once, he was at a loss for words.

Picard smiled warmly. "Call it . . . an extended loan. Since you lost your ship while saving ours, it seemed only fair to supply you with another one."

The older man grunted appreciatively. "It was a fine thought."

"I agree," the captain replied. "Unfortunately, I cannot take credit for it. It was actually Counselor Troi's idea."

"Actually," said the empath, "it was Ensign Kane's. Let us give credit where credit is due."

Scott looked at her. "Ah, lass." He took her hands in his. "Can ye ever forgive me fer the way I spoke to you?"

"Oh," she said, smiling impishly, "I don't know. Perhaps with time, I'll get over it."

"I'm sure ye will," Scotty told her, returning her smile. "I'm sure ye will."

Riker slapped the shuttle's metal skin. "She's not much to look at," he commented, "and she's not as roomy as a starship. Or even a transport, for that matter."

"Lad," said Scotty, "every woman has her own charms and her own beauty. Ye just have to know where to look."

Geordi leaned close to his fellow engineer. "It's a little slow, you know. But it'll get you to the Norpin Five colony." He paused. "That is, if that's where you really want to go."

Scotty considered the ship . . . and very slowly, a change came over his features. He seemed different. Rejuvenated, Geordi thought.

Turning to La Forge, Scott smiled his brightest smile yet. "The Norpin Five colony is where old men go to retire, laddie. Maybe I'll end up there someday —but not just yet."

"Oh?" said Picard. "Where do you intend to go?"

Scotty held out his hands. "Yer guess is as good as mine, Captain. There's still a lot I want to see." He indicated Data with a tilt of his head. "Fer example, the place my friend here came from."

"It is not difficult to find," the android assured him.

"And a million other places," the older man finished. He took a breath, let it out. "In fact," he said, "I think I'd best be off."

"So soon?" asked Crusher.

Scotty nodded. "And dinnae be tellin' me I need to

stay and rest up, Doctor. Any more of *this* sort of rest and they'll be carrying me out on a stretcher." He tilted his head. "Thouh ye're *still* the prettiest physician I ever saw."

Picard held out his hand. "I cannot convince you to stay awhile?"

"Nae likely," Scotty told him, taking the captain's hand and pressing it with great enthusiasm. "There's too much to see, and nae nearly enough time to see it in."

The captain nodded. "I understand. Bon voyage, Mr. Scott."

"Thank you, sir." He winked. "For everything."

A flurry of good-byes followed, with everyone present extending their warmest wishes. Scotty shook hands with several of them. He even hugged Counselor Troi. It did Geordi's heart good to see his partner so happy.

When it was all over, Scotty took his arm and escorted him out of earshot. Glancing back at the others, he said: "They're a good crew."

Geordi nodded. "Yeah."

Scott cast a last look around the shuttlebay. "And she's a fine ship, this *Enterprise*. A credit to her name." A pause. "But I've always found that a ship is only as good as the engineer who takes care of her. And from what I can see, she couldnae be in better hands." He chuckled. "Not even if *I* were in charge."

Geordi clapped Scott on the shoulder. "Better get a move on," he said. "Before the captain changes his mind."

"Aye," said Scott. "I've heard that's a captain's prerogative."

Getting into the shuttle, he shut the space door behind him. Geordi watched as he started the engine and gave them all a high sign. Then, as Picard himself worked the console to open the bay doors, Scotty nudged the shuttle to the brink of space—where an invisible force field separated the atmosphere in the shuttlebay from the ether.

Geordi could almost see the look in Scotty's eyes. It was all out there, everything he could ever want. And maybe some day, he'd even find some of those old friends he'd lost track of. Spock, for instance. And McCoy. And some of the others who were still around seventy-five years later.

Of course, there was uncertainty out there as well. And disappointment, maybe. But that came with the territory.

Suddenly, as Picard made the necessary adjustments in the force field, the shuttle took off. Geordi looked on with mixed emotions as it diminished with distance, finally banking and setting a course for only Scotty knew where. Geordi knew he'd miss Scotty and the elder engineer's stories, about everything from hang gliding to tribbles. But he was happy, very happy, for his friend.

For once again, Montgomery Scott was flying free.

ENTER A NEW GALAXY OF ADVENTURE
WITH THESE EXCITING

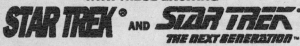

STAR TREK® AND **STAR TREK**® *THE NEXT GENERATION*™

TRADE PAPERBACKS FROM POCKET BOOKS:

THE STAR TREK COMPENDIUM by Alan Asherman.
The one must-have reference book for all STAR TREK fans, this book includes rare photos, behind the scenes production information, and a show-by-show guide to the original television series.

THE STAR TREK INTERVIEW BOOK by Alan Asherman.
A fascinating collection of interviews with the creators and stars of the original STAR TREK and the STAR TREK films.

MR. SCOTT'S GUIDE TO THE ENTERPRISE by Shane Johnson. An exciting deck-by-deck look at the inside of the incredible U.S.S. *Enterprise*™, this book features dozens of blueprints, sketches and photographs.

THE WORLDS OF THE FEDERATION by Shane Johnson.
A detailed look at the alien worlds seen in the original STAR TREK television series, the STAR TREK films, and STAR TREK: THE NEXT GENERATION — with a full-color insert of STAR TREK's most exotic alien creatures!

STAR TREK: THE NEXT GENERATION TECHNICAL MANUAL by Rick Sternbach and Michael Okuda. The long-awaited book that provides a never before seen look inside the U.S.S. *Enterprise* 1701-D and examines the principles behind STAR TREK: THE NEXT GENERATION's awesome technology — from phasers to warp drive to the holodeck.

THE KLINGON DICTIONARY by Mark Okrand. Finally, a comprehensive sourcebook for Klingon language and syntax—includes a pronunciation guide, grammatical rules, and phrase translations. The only one of its kind!

All Available from Pocket Books

POCKET
B O O K S